Praise for

VOICES OF THE LOST

Winner of the International Prize for Arabic Fiction

'Emotionally punchy.'

THE SUNDAY TIMES, 'BEST TRANSLATED FICTION FOR FEBRUARY 2021'

'Spare and deep, *Voices of the Lost* captivates. Hoda Barakat is one of Lebanon's greatest gifts to literature, and Booth allows her English audience to explore this painful and irresistible present.'

AMY BLOOM, AUTHOR OF *WHITE HOUSES*

'Extraordinary... Drawing on the power of testimonial ⸺ da Barakat's characters relate tales of loss, regret, and displace⸺ ⸺lly written and filled with a raw, audacious honesty ⸺ ⸺tters draw readers into an extraordinary em⸺

DIANA ⸺ *RADISE*

'Hoda Barakat is one of the ⸺ ⸺ovelists in the Arab world. Here, in a fugue o⸺ ⸺ ⸺ne etches the portraits of a series of existential refuge⸺ ⸺ween countries, languages, and lives.'

MARILYN HACKER, AUTHOR OF *BLAZONS*

'A subversive novel that examines sorrow, longing, violence, kindness, and compassion. The places may be named, but the protagonists are nameless. We love them because they are us.'

FADY JOUDAH, AUTHOR OF *TETHERED TO STARS*

'An astonishing novel... It is a fierce, challenging exploration of the extremities of rootlessness and desperation, rendered in a shocking clarity of voice.'

LEILA ABOULELA, AUTHOR OF *BIRD SUMMONS*

'Hoda Barakat's new novel reveals to us the many faces of power, war, love and despair as destinies mysteriously intersect, and all certainties are shaken. Through these letters, we glimpse the hidden story of immigration: characters condemned to suffer for nothing more than being born in the wrong place.'

JOKHA ALHARTHI, AUTHOR OF *CELESTIAL BODIES*,
WINNER OF THE MAN BOOKER INTERNATIONAL PRIZE

HODA BARAKAT

VOICES
of the
LOST

Translated by Marilyn Booth

ONEWORLD

A Oneworld Book

First published in Great Britain, the Republic of Ireland and Australia
by Oneworld Publications, 2021
Reprinted, 2021

First published in Arabic as *Barîd al layl* by Dar al Adab, Beirut,
Lebanon. Published by arrangement with The Raya Agency
for Arabic Literature and Rocking Chair Books Ltd.

Copyright © Hoda Barakat, 2017, 2021
English translation copyright © Marilyn Booth, 2021

The moral right of Hoda Barakat to be identified as the
Author of this work has been asserted by her in accordance
with the Copyright, Designs and Patents Act 1988

ISBN 978-1-78607-722-6
eISBN 978-1-78607-723-3

Typeset by Tetragon, London
Printed and bound in Great Britain by Clays Ltd, Elcograf S.p.A.

This is a work of fiction. While, as in all fiction, the literary perceptions and
insights are based on experience, all names, characters, places, and incidents
either are products of the author's imagination or are used fictitiously.

Oneworld Publications
10 Bloomsbury Street
London WC1B 3SR
United Kingdom

Stay up to date with the latest books,
special offers, and exclusive content from
Oneworld with our newsletter

Sign up on our website
oneworld-publications.com

MIX
Paper from
responsible sources
FSC
www.fsc.org
FSC® C018072

The night last night was strange and shaken:
More strange the change of you and me.
Once more, for the old love's love forsaken,
We went out once more toward the sea.

ALGERNON CHARLES SWINBURNE,
'AT A MONTH'S END'

PART ONE

Those Who are Lost

Dear

Since letters must always begin with Dear, then Dear it is.

I've never written a letter in my life. Not a single one. There was a letter in my mind, which I brooded over for years, rewriting it in my head again and again. But I never wrote it down. After all, my mother could hardly read, and so I expect she would have taken my letter to one of the village men with enough education to read it to her. That would have been a disaster, though! And anyway, then I learned that the village had flooded when the dam collapsed. The whole village was under water.

I don't know where the villagers went, or whether they were moved to another place. It was the latest thing in technology, the dam the president had ordered to be built to water the lands that had turned into desert. I've probably told you the story of the dam. I don't remember now, and that's not the issue anyway. No, my issue, more or less, is the letter that was circling inside my head for so long. What I always meant to do, you see, was to write to my mother about that moment when she dumped me on the train, all by myself. I was eight or nine years old. She gave me one loaf of bread and two boiled eggs. She said my uncle would be waiting for me in the city. She told me it was my job to get myself educated because I was the cleverest brother. 'Don't be afraid,' she said. 'Don't cry.'

But I have to admit that I was afraid. I was terrified. Alone in the world, as wild and aggressive as a little animal, ready to lash out – that's how I felt the minute the train started moving. I wanted desperately to hurt someone; I wanted it to be someone I didn't know, so I wouldn't be faced with making excuses for them, and be tempted to stop. Someone I had no connection with at all, and then I could do whatever I felt like doing without any interference from my mind. Sometimes I get the feeling that my mind is my greatest enemy.

As the train lurched into motion, a darkness came over me, like the dreary gloom of a midwinter sunset. No, I wasn't afraid in that moment, and I didn't cry. I simply felt myself sinking into the sour odour of eggs boiled hours before. I wanted to toss them away but I didn't dare. It was still very early in the morning – so early that it had taken my mother some force to rouse me. But it didn't get any lighter. The train kept moving through an unchanging half-light, as if it were in a long tunnel with no opening at the other end.

That winter twilight lived on in my head, whatever the hour of the day. It was the darkness that falls when the sun vanishes on the horizon, the darkness that invariably makes children cry and fills true romantics with sadness – those well-meaning romantics, from Egypt's Ihsan Abdel Quddous to Germany's Rainer Maria Rilke. Melancholy seizes the gentle, good beings in the world and there's no explaining its grip. When the child psychologist writes about this, she says: 'Mothers, do not let these six o'clock crying spells alarm you. They're only a test. A child knows instinctively that, alone and abandoned by its mother, it will certainly die. The child's sobs are a call, a way to assure itself that its mother is still in the world. That she is here, and because she is here it will not die.' But she – my mother – was not there. In that moment, and from then on, she was not there.

Because you are a romantic woman and you grow sad with the sunset, and because you like getting letters written on real paper, which the postman carries in a leather bag hung on his shoulder all the way to your little metal post box, I will write you a letter. It is sure to be the only letter of my entire life, sent or received. And because this miserable sleet, half-snow, half-rain, has not let up since dawn, I will stay at home. I won't go out in this weather. And I will write you a letter.

Now I have to find something to fill the lines on this empty white page. I wonder what I can tell you that's new, when it hasn't been very long since we last met. But maybe more time has passed than I think? And, well, I don't have a gift for turning news into stories. I never tell anyone anything very useful or interesting. People only listen to what others say because they are nosy. I talk a lot, and I go on talking as long as I can see that spark of inquisitiveness in my listener's eyes, telling me he's seeking out some juicy story that he thinks I might have. It won't let go of me, this need to relay information, or my need won't let go of whoever it is we've agreed to smear behind his back, my listener and I. Spiteful gossip – though we call it by other names.

By now you've realized, most likely, that everything I say is just the product of the moment, whatever happens to come out when I open my mouth. Like, I'm sitting in the café and in front of me I can see a man perched on a wooden chair, so I launch into a long commentary on the history of woodworking and what the differences are between one variety of wood and another, and the particular ways each kind is used. And then I might move on to the harm that's being done to our planet's forests, how love of the hamburger is denuding them and turning them into arid plains, how it is all part of the vicious greed that fuels savage capitalism and our vast multinational companies and governments, and so forth and so on. If the fellow across from me is sitting on a plastic chair, then I dive into the world of plastic, from the history of its invention as a petroleum by-product to its latest uses in the most advanced operating theatres, and on to the unique role plastics play in the world of molecular medicine, et cetera, et cetera.

I have learned a lot since the village train station vanished behind me. I crammed my head (which my mother claimed was so clever and quick) full of things, and I did it with insatiable greed and persistence. I couldn't be stopped. Collecting information became an urgent need. I wanted to know anything and everything, in whatever field it might be. That's because I had empty spaces to fill, cryptic hollows like those of bulimia or addiction, where there is no explanation, no memory of *why*. And then – well, I might as well make the most of this storage vault of mine. Let me use my bank of knowledge to baffle my listener into silence. And why not use all of these words I have to stun women? To stun you, for example. I don't give your mind any chance to wander free because I'm so afraid that then you might stop and think. Because I don't want to hear – I'm not interested in hearing – anything more about you than I knew instantly in the first moment I saw you. The other reason I won't stop talking is that I don't want to crack open a window that lets any closeness in. Intimacy is a trap. Words muttered in lowered voices between two heads bowed close together, the confession-talk people use to break their isolation, to keep away the loneliness that crouches in the hearts of sensitive creatures who can't stand solitude, or… A trap, a *warta* in the original sense of the word: a dark chasm reaching deep into the earth. That's according to the dictionary. Fancy that!

OK, about me. By now you've realized that nothing of that sort ever happens to me – or happens with me. No emotions! Unless it's something along the lines of the hell I gave that plumber. He gave me an appointment and I waited all day but he never showed up. But I'm not even very entertaining when it comes down to it, and I won't be able to, or wouldn't have been able to, keep you interested. I find myself repeating stupid trivial bits of information that I've already told you, and it bores you to hear them again. So you begin making an effort to avoid showing how bored you are, hearing them over and over, and then I begin making an effort to avoid showing that I know you're bored, hearing them over and over. And so it goes. But when I start again, boring you once more with all my words, actually I'm telling you something. I'm letting you know that this is all I have to offer. No hidden depths, no inner realm. So why would you stick with me? What do you find in me? With me? What do you find there?

I know I'm a man of average looks; perhaps even that's a bit of an exaggeration. And I can be somewhat impolite, or rough-mannered… Let's just say that I lack polish. Like when I phone you at the last minute to cancel our date. I tell you I'm sleepy and I don't want to go out. But I don't even invite you to come round here instead. Calculating the time as precisely as I do, I know as I'm talking to you that you've probably already dressed and got completely ready to go out. I excuse myself with several loud yawns and hang up before we've made another plan to meet. Why wouldn't you leave me?

Without punishing me in any way, without so much as a cross word, you show up at our next date. Your heart as big as ever, you bring your head close to mine after our routine little kisses on the cheek. You look me in the eye, and when you blink slowly and then open your eyes wider to focus on me, it's to show me that you really mean it when you ask, 'How are you?' If it looked like you were just trying to open the door to a little seduction, I would have an answer ready. 'I haven't been sleeping very well,' I would tell you. But that would just be for the sake of keeping our conversation going for a pleasant hour or so, exchanging scraps of conversation about sleep and insomnia, the secrets in our dreams, and our waking fantasies about whatever.

Soon, though, I see you circling closer, insistently, obstinately even, buzzing like a fly in the cloud of carbon dioxide that I let out with each breath.

You want something else, something more. You want me to complain, to you and you alone, about the reasons why I can't sleep. Insomnia offers you a little crack in my defences that you think you can widen and then enter. If you come at me this way, you think, I might start revealing things. But why do you need all of these games? Why, when you can see so easily how smitten I am! How I break into a sweat and start breathing hard as soon as you come near enough that I catch the fragrance of your neck, sniffing at it like a baby animal. Your beauty is so radiant that it could burn me to ashes. You don't need me in order to know how powerfully attractive you are. It's enough for you to see that desire in other men's eyes. Of course, you know this perfectly well, and it's because you're so sure in that knowledge that you always humour me like this. Someone in your position has no need of anxiety, or self-doubt, or jealousy.

Sometimes you are so confident in the power you hold over men, and exude it so spectacularly, that I have to distance myself. Perhaps we're in bed; so I pick up a book. Or I ask you if you remember that gorgeous woman we encountered one time when we were together, winking at you as I speak, as if we're guys strutting our manhood, as if I'm just reviewing my seduction skills, how easy it is to pick up pretty women. You just laugh along with me, like you're in on the joke, without showing any anger or even the least irritation. Then you leave.

It's not good enough to show regret. Help me. You need to be a little more modest. Less showy. Not modest to the point of lowering yourself, only far enough to let me know you're a little attached to me. I assume there's no need to remind you that I grew up without a family. My father was lost to me. He fell out of the picture, maybe from nothing more than sheer neglect. As if that woman flung him out of the train window as she was flinging me inside the train.

I don't know how men love women. In my village, which was wiped out by the collapsed dam, there were no women who loved or were loved. There were just sexless creatures. Or I was at an age then when sex didn't yet exist. But I do remember being ashamed of my relentless hunger, and how constantly occupied I was with trying to hide or disguise it. The only time I could forget about it was when I was at school or studying. The other boys were always swarming around, in the house or in the street, tens of them, like flies, sometimes like clouds of stinging wasps. At best, like flying cockroaches. There was nowhere to escape to. Nowhere to begin carving out a manhood, or a womanhood. Nowhere for any luxuries of that sort.

I recall very little of that place and the people there, and what I do remember makes me sick to my stomach. Even when it comes back to me in dreams, it's all more like a nightmare. These are places eaten away by the mange. Leper colonies. They disintegrate, falling into pieces, falling from the memory as a leper's fingers and toes fall away from his body. Arid, brittle places sick with poverty and need, long past the opportunity for redemption.

Whenever I read something about how comforting it is
to remember one's childhood – all that innocence, the
tenderness it arouses within you – my head swims. My
nostrils fill with the stink of muddy dung heaps until I
can't breathe; my eyes cloud over with a film of dust,
gummed together with that thick, persistent infectious
pus that I do remember. You would need a lot more clean
water than we ever had to rinse off enough of the pus to
be able to force open your eyelids even for a moment,
for maybe an hour or two before the flies returned in
swarms, attacking and destroying, raking across your
face almost as though they have claws. They were so
used to being slapped away that it didn't faze them. Is
this the kind of thing you want to know? My childhood?
Those years that we were taught to believe provide the
entire bedrock of personality, from adolescence and
beyond, the basis for the man I am today? Those happy
years of one's early life, because, of course, it's always
got to be a *happy childhood*, right?

You come back to the issue of my insomnia, taking
advantage of the only opening that's been offered to
you. Is this all I will get for myself, this questioning of
yours? 'You're still not sleeping well?' you ask. 'Did you
take my advice? That herbal infusion I told you to take,
did you really drink it? All of it?' OK, then why not go
further? Why don't you go on to make some allusion

13

to the insomnia of lovers, for example? Isn't this what you're really getting at? Fine. But whatever it was that kept me awake last night isn't what will keep me from sleeping tonight.

So. Either I must be lying in order to avoid blurting out some revelation that would be truly intimate – and so you hammer at me even more – or I'm holding back a lie that's on the tip of my tongue, and if so, it must be because I am an anxiety-ridden, unstable person, and there you are, just poised to hurry to my rescue. Or I've changed my mind and now I don't feel any urgency about keeping your attention fixed on me and my insomnia, and all the rest.

Why does it never occur to you that the reason for my insomnia might, in fact, be *you*? Like, why haven't you ever tried to yank me back when you can see I'm absorbed in some other woman who seems to be chasing the sleep from my eyes? Just for instance?

Frankly, I can't stand it any longer – this need of yours to search for meanings in everything. You've become just like the stories in those books you read: beginning, middle, and everything wrapped up neatly at the end. An ironclad triangular logic. You've become terrifying in your devious cleverness, your attempts to wrench my insides out of me, with the pure joy of a hunter on the point of disembowelling his prey. Victorious, he flashes his weapon, ready to begin slicing from the lowest point of the belly even before the heart has stopped beating and while there's still a stir of breath coming from the victim's slack jaws.

Yes, of course I'm exaggerating! That's precisely because you always insist on taking words literally, with absolute seriousness, as if they're a document submitted as evidence in court. Because one day I used the word *unique*, I guess. I said there was nobody like you in my world. But any run-of-the-mill woman, even one without much intelligence, would immediately consign words like that to the little box marked 'silliest and most banal male seduction techniques'. It is true that I also said, on one occasion, that I was completely crazy about you. All right. As if no man has ever been crazy about you before! As if I am the only man on this planet! You lowered your eyelids and smiled like a practised flirt, not forgetting to add a little touch of confused embarrassment. You didn't say anything. You didn't say, 'I'm crazy about you too.' Then…well, then you began waiting for the story to begin.

Which story do you want, my child? Wasn't that 'confession' of mine enough for you? Even the folktale hero

15

Clever Hasan had to have it explained to him in *One Thousand and One Nights*: what he had to do to win the princess, Sitt al-Husn, the Lady of Goodness and Beauty! And it was only after he followed instructions that the little fish with the precious gemstone in its gut jumped into his lap. So, my Sitt al-Husn, is that what you want? Do I have to go and catch some fish? Or do you want me to sing to you like the crooner Farid al-Atrash with his weepy ballads? It seems we've got ourselves into a terrible misunderstanding and

Wait a minute.

There's a man over there who won't stop looking in my direction. He comes out onto the balcony, his eyes already trained on me. He's been standing there behind the glass, staring at me, facing me and looking straight at me, just standing there, on and on.

This is really getting to me. I've tried waving at him to get him to stop, to go away. I've tried to make him realize I'm not a customer of any of the lowlifes around here. No doubt, given his constant surveillance of me, or almost constant anyway, he must have seen you here at my place; he must have been watching as we pulled the curtain shut in his face. This isn't rational, what he is doing, and it isn't all right. The curtain blocks my one source of light, and I don't want to have to keep it permanently drawn to be rid of the sight of him. If I do that, I might as well shout out loud that I'm afraid. That I fear him and I'm hiding from him. Even when I turn off the light, keeping a surreptitious eye on him, I find him still there, looking in my direction, a wicked little smile lifting his heavy moustache. As if he can see me even when I'm hiding in here, in the dark.

So how would you explain this? Would you shrug it off as nothing more than my mad ravings? Would you say it's just the typical paranoia of a cokehead? Do you really believe I'm addicted? Because you thought I was admitting it when I gave in after you begged and begged me to stop ruining my health? It amazes me – my little doll! – to see how remote you can be from what goes on in real life. All right, fine, the cocaine isn't 'real life'. But these ready-made ideas you go on about! When you know nothing at all about what real people are doing, except what you pick up here and there. About how people should or should not live. About how things should or should not be.

None of this would bother me much if only you hadn't taken it so far. If only you didn't swallow me up. Whenever I take a step back, you push forward to occupy the space I've left there. Even this furnished room: like you, I've begun to call it 'the house' or even 'home'. But it's just a miserable room in a block of flats where pimps rent space for the prostitutes who strut up and down the street below us. Fine, no problem – we'll call it a 'home'. Because, after all, these intentions you have, about lifting me up, out of the ranks of poor men – including the business of your 'forgetting' that money you left on the table – they're good intentions, of course. Except that I'm not a poor man, I'm just broke. But my intelligence, as you say, is wealth! Fine, good. Then you come in lugging these cleaning liquids and disinfectants and various cloths and wipes and rags, and storage cartons and carrier bags and... Like the white tornado in the TV commercial, you go about sweeping and dusting and polishing and picking up, saying you want to make this pitiful room into a home.

What?!

And since you seem to be in a state of tornado-bliss that begs description, how can I object? There's no law that says a liberated woman has to embrace filth and chaos, true enough. But you couldn't help noticing that the clean sheets and the smells of Dettol and those other disinfectants had an effect on my performance. I couldn't come as fast or as hard. So you pulled back from making further attacks on the tiny space into which I've crept as a refuge from the world. You promised to leave things alone, to let it all return to the state it was in before the tornado slammed down. But you didn't even have to do that. I was beginning on my own to change the sheets and empty the kitchen sink and dust everything in sight whenever I expected you to show up. That's how frightened I was of you! As if the only thing left undone was to clear a little alcove for our love child and begin assembling the stylish wood-framed baby bed we'd have picked out together from the Ikea catalogue!

You are so distanced from ordinary life. So unconnected to it. One time you said – I think you were only half joking – that your period was late.

What is it you want? Do you really want to be a mother?

To be my mother?

I've wondered what it is about this role that could possibly entice you. Is it your hormones, which rise into your head and fog your vision? Aren't you supposed to be a civilized person who has control over her instincts? What about that cherished speech of yours on abused femininity? Was that just a trap you set to reassure me? Make up your mind, and then give me a chance to

explain to you – maybe adding in a few details but not
too many – where that rural train took me. What I mean
by *where* is this: how was it that I forgot the woman who
dumped me on that train, and forgot her so quickly? I
must have done, because otherwise how could I have
stayed on the train that was taking me somewhere far
away and completely unknown? I forgot her immediately. And she forgot me too. She never came to see
me, not even once. Maybe she thought it would help
me immerse myself in my studies. The only thing her
ignorance and backwardness left me with was the odour
of boiled eggs and that dark, dark tunnel. If they had
lined up a bunch of women in front of me and placed
her among them, I wouldn't have known her from the
next one. That woman shattered my life and made me
a fugitive in God's wide world, in a world where everyone was a stranger. A world of strangers, exiles and
orphans. I never heard even a hint that she made any
attempt to find me.

All that happened was that, when she died, one of my
brothers found out my telephone number – I have no
idea how. He said, 'I am your brother So-and-So.' I don't
even recall now which brother it was. Then he said,
'Your mother has died.' I think I remember respond-
ing automatically, 'May your life be long', or something
suitable like that. And then, suddenly, I was furiously

20

angry. Why did they even contact me? I asked myself. What did they think they were doing, phoning me, when they'd never bothered to do that before? Like, even just to ask how I was, for example.

When the hen was ailing, my mother cared for it, carrying it around all day long to keep it out of range of the roosters' pecking. She fed it grain from her own hand, and she didn't leave it on its own until it had made a full recovery. She said prayers for the ewe that had a hard time giving birth, staying close and stroking its neck, singing to it, and then trilling with loud joy when she could see the baby lamb moving in the placenta. She used to sob at the sound of the lambs bleating when they were newly weaned from their mother's milk. All of those creatures – but not me. There were days on end when she didn't even look in my direction. She would tip hot water over my head and then scream at me when I wailed. Me – I was no use. I couldn't give her anything. No eggs, no milk, no meat. I was nothing but an empty belly beneath a wide-open mouth. And then she got rid of me, sending me away to a place she didn't know anything about.

So. She was dead. There was no longer any space for manoeuvre – no room for revenge, no chance to settle the accounts once and for all. No reason to go back there, which in any case had happened only in my darkest fantasies. In those nightmares I watched myself working out a simple way to tell her how all the oxytocin cells in my brain had flickered out. I would explain to her that, here, the doctors call this brain matter 'the bonding molecule', since she had some respect for book-learning and science. I would tell her that in *my* brain, which supposedly was a cut above my brothers' brains, there were regions an X-ray would show as a void, completely extinguished, no longer reachable by any electron charges or rays. These are precisely the regions of the brain that manage depression, fear, violence and feelings of abandonment.

I read in some book that mother animals eat their male young out of sheer attachment. I read about how a mother swallows her infant son, returning him to her womb, because she knows the infant male will always be wretched unless he's with her. She returns him to the place of ultimate contentment, which no other state of bliss can ever resemble. She, whose organs are nourished only by her baby's masculine self, will make her sacrificial offering upon his beloved corpse. There it is, the love that devours even corpses.

As for me, my mother dumped me on the country train as though I were a sack of rubbish. That's why, at first, I accepted your little sport, those sudden intervals when you played at being a mother-in-miniature whose milk I could breathe in as I tried to become a true male. I tried hard, and I went on trying, but it was just not possible. I was like a person who keeps on walking straight ahead even when he can see the cliff edge and the chasm beyond it opening out clearly in front of him. It got to the point where I couldn't come close to your breasts without thinking immediately of milk, and I was afraid, if I squeezed them, of white drops running onto my hands and the rancid smell that stream of white liquid would leave on me.

But it was when I caught the smell of garlic in this 'home' that I decided you really had gone too far, and you had to be stopped. That we needed a thorough stock-taking. For you to fry eggs or open a tin of sardines, fine. But garlic? Garlic means *cooking*. It means: *I'm here and I'm staying*, and there is no convincing response to that. Who can stand up to a woman who is ready to kiss a mouth reeking of garlic? A woman who embraces a man's most odious smells, and is happy to wash his undergarments or his smelly socks? Who defies a mother knowing full well that she means to consume him?

I think… I think the time has come when I have to speak to this man who hasn't stopped looking in my direction. Maybe we can come to an understanding. I'll tell him something like this: Look. Frankly speaking, I love women. What I mean is: I only love women. But I don't have anything against homosexuals; in fact, I have some dear friends among the

If I find him willing to listen, I'll explain to him, calmly and gently, how I'm finding this really annoying – his watching me like this. How it is beginning to feel very, very annoying. I'll tell him that I could decide, however, that there's really no need to go to the police and inform them about the

I won't do it. I read in some book that there are homos whose lusts, if they're bottled up, can turn into criminal acts of extreme violence. Because those types can't control their urges. There's no limit to their sadism. Not even murder satisfies their sick inclinations. Many of them become serial killers. True, I read this in one of those cheap books that are pulped and sold by the kilo, but who knows. Who knows? The truth is, I'm afraid of my own shadow.

I'll wait. Maybe he'll get bored and just stop.

I wanted to ask you something. How can you take this overwhelming passion so lightly? This rare passion, the desire – my wanting sex with you over and over, tens of times, hundreds. Don't you sense that? How my chest feels like it is about to burst open and my heartbeat is going wild and I think I am suffocating? How I've submitted to all the moves of your body like a servant obeying his master, or maybe even a slave? How I kiss you from your toes all the way up to the ends of every lock of hair? How I study the length and breadth of your radiant skin, until I've committed to memory the location and the exact colour of the tiniest beauty mark so that I can see it perfectly with my eyes shut? How could you think it was somehow lacking, this passion? It's tragic. Yes, this really is a tragedy, because it is all I have to offer. A pure and overwhelming desire, full and complete and perfect. A desire that lacks nothing.

It's you who have taken away the perfection of my desire. You reduced its value with your incessant questions about 'guarantees' and 'sell-by dates' and so forth. How much longer are you going to…?

It's just an exam that never ends, isn't it, and you want me to fail. So, at that point, I'm going to give answers, because your insistence pushes me to it, but they're answers you don't want to hear. If that happens, and my answers really aren't the ones you want to hear, don't object! Here is what I say: that naturally – little by little and simply because this is the way things happen – we will find ourselves increasingly bored and irritated every time we're together. In other words, things will begin to take their natural course. They're already taking their natural course, I'll say. Eventually I'll go back to staring at other women's thighs and breasts, and I'll stop paying attention to your pleasant chitchat and your breasts, as near as they are. And when I say this to you, you just accept it! You fall for it, almost right away. That's why I have to keep pushing you into a corner, as far as I can make you go. I do it elaborately, I overdo it, so that maybe, just maybe, you'll protest, show some irritation, maybe even give a light rebuke. Next come my outright lies and inventions. Like telling you I can't see you for days ahead, or perhaps for weeks, because I'm...well, I'm busy. With what? With whom? But you won't even ask.

The next time I see you, after we've been out of touch for a bit, I'm startled to realize that the lies I've been telling are turning into the truth! It really is possible to live without you. I mean, these are the laws of nature after all. I haven't actually made anything up, and I didn't do anything to make this happen. Then, when I see you passing on the street, going the other way, home to your place, I might take a deep breath once you're behind me. I'll feel fine. I'll tell myself I'm not going to be jerked around by a woman I've been on top of. I'll turn up my jacket collar and keep walking briskly and lightly, in high spirits. A pretty girl, that one. A pleasant and fun girl, we had some nice times together.

Or. I might turn up my jacket collar and try to breathe deeply, but my sobs defeat me. I'll choke on my tears and shout, in Arabic so that no one can understand me, 'She would have got bored anyway. She would have got tired of me for sure, because there's nothing in me to keep a woman interested. That's why she got into that game, and she made me get into it too, that game of cooking, and turning the room into *home*. It's the law of nature, she was going to leave me anyway. And I couldn't have stood that.'

I feel so sad, really sad, as I'm writing to you about all of this – my indecision, my ups and downs between the relief of shrugging you off and the tragedy of losing you, the two of us a failure together.

But…but how can this man have the strength to stand out there in the cold all this time? Or does he go inside and shut the balcony door behind him whenever I move out of his sight? As if he can appear, through a wizard's magic, when I turn on the light or open the curtain, and only then. He looks a little bit like that nasty man we came upon one day in the supermarket in the city centre. You commented at the time on how ugly you found his bushy moustache, and his insolent stares and…and then I couldn't help displaying you as if you were my 'booty', goods I owned, as dictated by the language of testosterone. You know, sometimes your good looks play against you. They rouse my animal instincts: my horns come out, my hooves paw at the ground and as the cloud of dust rises, I snort into it. Just because I show all this jealousy doesn't mean I'm in love with you. It's a thing between males, competition over the size of one's balls, and it has nothing to do with the particular female who happens to be standing in this territory occupied by two random males. It is in my genes. Given my struggle with the world, the whole world, I have no intention of fighting my own genes too.

Why am I at war with the whole world? I don't know. Ask the world! Maybe it's because of the feeling I always have that I'm in the middle of combat but I don't have any weapons at all. And every time I venture out of my hiding place, I come back covered with bruises and wounds. It's not that I'm particularly peaceful, and it's not that I'm surrendering, it's just that I can't find any means of arming myself. The real disaster is my weak constitution. I don't dare strike anyone. So that's it. I'm weak, and I'm a coward, and that doubles the rage I feel when I look at myself.

You complain sometimes about my aggressive behaviour, especially since you can't find any reason for it. You question me about the motivations for my anger, not because you want to ease it away through your love for me – all we have to do is to slip between the sheets for my anger to leave me – but because you are nosy, and you're working on your tactics, ready for a new attack.

Do you remember the first time I saw you?

You reminded me of actresses from the 1940s. That's what I told you. What I meant by it, of course, was that I found you gorgeous. When you didn't respond, not even with a smile, I told myself you had won the first round and you would pay a high price for it. Ever since you first came into my bed, and every time I came out of you, I would take a deep breath and gather my forces, with all the effort this took, to play the role I had decided on for myself. Caressing your hair, I would ask, 'Was it *good*?' In other words, did our little 'turn' bring you pleasure? Is that how you like it? As if I were the plumber who asks the lady of the house whether the job he's just finished suits her taste.

I throw you in with all those ordinary women, the whole degraded lot of them. Saying that helps me to put you at a distance, telling you jokes I've told you many times before. Or I go and stand at the window and comment on 'the weather out there', to remind you of the *out-there*, to remind you that you have to go, before staying here makes you late. I get dressed to see you out, even if just a very little way, acting like a *gentleman*. It hurts me, deep inside, that you make no objections to my disgraceful behaviour. You don't show any anger. You don't scold me, or swear at me. And then you come back to me as though nothing at all happened, as though you don't care. Damn you! How can you accept it? Why don't you love me? Damn you to hell!

When I hit you that first time, and your immediate response was to put your arms around me, I knew that freeing myself of you was going to be harder than I thought. The next day I said to you – I was trying to find an excuse for myself – that I didn't know what you expected from me. Crying a little, you replied that you didn't expect anything at all. At all? Really? Nothing at all? How can it be, then, that you give the appearance of someone clutching an empty pitcher and circling me, coming closer and closer each time, and I have no idea what I could possibly fill your pitcher with?

Do you believe that I'm hiding stories from you, secrets I'm keeping only for myself? If so, why do you come back? Do you really not pick up on the fact that I'm making no effort to hide my relationships with other women from you? Or do you figure that I'm singling you out as someone special precisely because I do tell you about them? That I'm choosing you above everyone else? I'm letting you into an intimacy that none of the others share? Or is this about your avant-garde views, your rejection of the whole idea that any one body could own another? That is, it doesn't concern you whether my body is all yours. Fine, so be it. You will not knock on my door, then, nor will you go on knocking until I open it. You won't chase away the woman you might find in my bed and then work as hard as you can to get me back. You won't pull my head to your breast and rub it ever so gently. Why are you so hard? And then, if you are this hard, how can you take seriously my regret and the tears I shed after hitting you?

Despite all your pretences and claims, you give the impression of having just arrived from some ancient century. From some barren and paltry era, where embalmed, pale, consumptive women are made to stand on balconies, pressed together and indistinguishable in the neon of an ice-cold moon, like frozen fish packed in a carton. In a time when other women were sucking

31

out the blood of the long-awaited knight on his steed in order to transform him into someone else, pumping fire-water into his skull, smearing his white horse with kohl and thick, coloured powders, and then bursting into laughter at the sight.

In fact, you aren't even particularly conscious of my existence unless I am standing in front of you, and alone. You don't realize, for instance, that when you laugh out loud at the words of another man, I want to slap you. 'I'll do it later,' I tell myself. 'When we are alone. And I'll explain it to her. I'll tell her it's only that I have a jealous sense of protection towards her because these men who cluster around her deserve nothing but scorn.' Not because I have any fear of them or because I dread what they might be able to do. No, not at all. But it's ridiculous, the way you humour those types.

Do you really have such an absurd need for diversion? Why? Is it because I'm boring? Irritating? Can't you see, with those pretty eyes of yours, how I'm burning with desire when I kiss you down there?

At least that must be some kind of diversion. No? You don't understand this passion. And every time I've made love to you, I've regretted it. I ask myself, 'What business do I have with this woman? My desire gives her a power I can't stand.'

When I have dreams about you at night, I wake up in terror, as if I've had a truly frightening nightmare. My first thought is that I've lost my ability to perform, and immediately I'm certain I've lost it for good. I go on a mad search for you and when I find you, I'm desperate to prove that nightmare accusation wrong, and then to show how silly and unimportant this relationship between us is. In the café I don't have much to say. I yawn, and I just say over and over how much I regret the poor circumstances that don't allow us to meet more often. And naturally, you will look at your watch, leaving me to flail about in the swamp of my own potency. I entice you to stay a little longer, and you believe I might reveal something important to you. Then I look at my watch. I leave you sitting there in the café as I hurry outside, excusing myself abruptly for having not paid attention to the time. Walking on in the fresh air, I buy bread and some fruit. I try to imagine you returning home in a state of irritation, asking yourself what pushed me to insist so forcefully on seeing you? Then I imagine you going out to meet your friends, and I throw the bread and fruit into the nearest rubbish bin and climb the stairs empty-handed and cold. I might stop off to see one of my girlfriends or bring her home with me, rustling up a quick supper, a good one accompanied by constant banter and some

Since, after all, I am not really up to your standard, and since I reject the whole idea of standards and propriety, and no one ever taught me how to behave according to its rules.

Sometimes, alone at night, I'm in torment, haunted by your face, which I can't rid myself of. I can't stop imagining the sad expression you wear, which pursues me like a demon. And it's all because of me. Your face, lonely without me. It agonizes me that I have no place for you – that you don't have a place here with me, and then that you are so accepting about staying outside.

But you're right to be that way. What life could I invite you into? I'm broke, totally broke, face in the mud. To others, I look like someone who refuses to accept what the fates have dealt me, since a person in my condition doesn't turn down work no matter how low the pay. Any wage, for someone like me, would be respectable, that's true enough. But the work? I did work, after all. I worked for that insurrectionist military man who started a newspaper because he wanted to instruct all of God's

creatures on the principles of democracy. Every time a
team of inspectors from the Ministry of Labour marched
in, he ordered all of our offices to be emptied. We had
to clump our way down the steps of his splendid palace
like a flock of bewildered sheep staggering onto the
boulevard. We waited, huddling in nearby cafés until
the guard came to sound the all-clear whistle. The
guard – the heavy, the big man's qabaday who handled
security. It was all because we were working without
papers, under the table. Black-market workers.

This lover of democracy who had fled his native land – or
who had probably worked out a deal with his 'historic'
zaeem, his old militia chief, that meant staying away
for a bit in the hope people would forget the massacres
he'd instigated – this lover of democracy gave us lec-
tures. He made us come to the palace he had bought
and renovated as a headquarters, so that he could lec-
ture us as if we were his students. He allowed himself
to congratulate us on living in exile, just as he was,
because we were freedom-seekers. Like him, we had
refused to accept the oppression and the backwardness
of our Arab nations.

Because we were seekers of freedom and democracy,
and foreigners here, if anyone attempted to apply for
residency, the qabaday accompanied them to the ground

35

floor where the quasi-secret office of investigations was. It was an investigations bureau in every sense of the word, with the authority to throw people out. All it took was a gesture to the qabaday: *Take this petty clerk to gather up his things in silence and see him out through the metal gates* (which, as a rule, were locked).

We did ask ourselves, we asked each other, how the ministry inspectors could explain to themselves all these unoccupied desks, bare except for scattered cups of coffee that were still hot. Money seals mouths, we concluded. Money creates delays. Money even overcomes the law. We said these things to each other, over and over, offering bitter condolences. That these were the necessary conditions of living in exile. That we were our countries' orphaned children. That our families were poor. We always promised each other that we would meet up and look for other work together.

It's strange that I never even once blew up at the qabaday. Somehow, and I don't know exactly why, I found this security fellow to be a good guy. We shared a lot of laughs, especially about the huge difference between his massive powerful physique and my body. He loved playing his strongman game – his muscle against men who wrote for a living. He must have asked himself how this writing business could possibly help any one of us to confront the kind of nerve someone like him lived by, with his strong heart and powerful brawn. He was like a child-giant, a baby-doll face over an inhumanly thick neck. He reminded us of certain relatives we had back in our villages, young men who boasted of their ability to lift heavy weights and fight bulls, who even pulled heavily laden wagons on their own as if they themselves were the animals. I found him entertaining and we talked a lot, but I never asked about his duties at the newspaper. To my good fortune, he never ushered me through those gates.

And me – a man broke to the point of humiliation – did I ever object or complain? Did I leave the work? No, I just trudged along like a donkey who tugs his own halter forward. Until we arrived one morning and began waiting, like migrant workers who show up hoping for day contracts. We pressed on the bell repeatedly and stared into the camera above it, hoping against hope that if we had been counted as tardy it would not be deducted from our wages. The gates remained closed. No one responded. We waited a long time. What was usually a quiet street was choked with people, because we were all out there. A voice came over the loudspeaker system. 'Go home, there is no work today.' The same thing happened several days in a row, until we gave up. None of us felt angry. Nobody tried for revenge against the zaeem who had stolen his country's wealth and smuggled drugs, the lover of democracy who had taken such obvious pleasure lecturing us and then having the sweets he had ordered passed around. We were all preoccupied with looking for other work, something similar to the work we had been expelled from, of course, something to tide us over for at least a few months. That's why we had to keep quiet, to appear obedient and compliant. Anyway, without any work contract, there was no way you could make a complaint.

The labour market we knew had dried up, after a few ventures of this sort failed. Or let us say that the money shifted to other markets. Little by little, the only choices were cocaine or the Islamists. And because I am a coward – a gutless coward, really – I was more comfortable with the first option. Many times, I went to the so-called 'Café National', and I offered my services, to carry suitcases and so forth. No one employed me. I stopped making the rounds of the cafés, but I didn't go anywhere near the Islamists, either. Signing up with them was out of the question. And anyway, if I'd failed with the traffickers, how then could I ever

Then it occurred to me to try renewing my passport. But that's when I got a shock: I was *persona non grata*. They held on to the passport. 'Fine, keep it!' I said. I wasn't trying to renew it in order to go back. I just wanted to extend my visa here, or perhaps move to some Arab city – Beirut or Amman, maybe. Then I began mulling over the question of how I could live here without a residence permit. An illegal immigrant who could not get any real work. It didn't seem possible.

That's how I found myself among 'the opposition'. I got labelled *opposition* after a French newspaper published an article I had translated from the Arabic. I didn't write it, I just translated it, and for a pitiful sum of money. Then I told myself that as long as this was how it was, I might as well really join the opposition. Maybe I would find people there who were in similar circumstances, and they might help me somehow. They had their networks, their connections, their ways.

But none of them would put up with me. As much as they fought among themselves, they were united on one thing: that I was 'suspicious'. I was just an opportunist out for my own gain, and they would have to keep a close eye on me until I came up with something they could all agree proved I was worthy and fit for service.

What more can I say?

Apart from all of that, I'm a backward soul. I'm aggressive, I'm violent, and then to top it off, I'm an addict. And also, my best sex fantasies begin with me pushing you into the arms of some other man, or men. You're naked, and sometimes you're underneath, sometimes on top. Most likely it is all a way of dealing with my jealousy. I like seeing you looking just like any other woman, your body alive with animal health and desire, moving from one set of hands to another, one mouth to another, all of them making your flesh glow and burn and open. To see you as just another woman, like my neighbour, the baker's wife, who laughs and writhes and squirms when I do something that hurts her, like when I slap her, and then she scampers off to stuff herself with food, when, just a few minutes before, she was squealing with pleasure. There's nothing more exquisite, nothing more primal, than those common, functional spaces where people can just get on with the shared acts they've been engaging in down through many ages, without singling anyone out, without any

Besides all that, I miss you.

Here I am again, spouting nonsense. All the cocaine in the market is contaminated. Except for the really expensive stuff, it's all tainted, diluted with paraceta-mol. Instead of puffing me up like a rooster, a long sniff of it sucks out whatever oxygen might still be in my head.

Why am I telling you all this?

Yes – to tell you how I got to this point, broke, with nothing, not even papers. This doesn't change anything about my relationship with you. I'm not writing to you now in order to bring you back. No, in fact it could be – this letter I'm writing, I mean – it could be the last thing I have to say. I'm not holding on to any illusions. I need to find a woman who's getting on a little in age, a widow, something like that, who wouldn't be unhappy to have me as a husband. First I could get residence papers, and then maybe even citizenship.

God, it's all so ridiculous. Most of my days are just one absurdity after another.

Forget what I've written in this letter. I just wanted to talk to you, to keep you in my head a little longer, because I miss you. My head is so confused, I get things so wrong and I don't know where I am, that I almost suspect some of what I've written was meant for another woman. Or maybe another man, someone I was imagining as a sort of twin, maybe. Something like that, anyway. Forget what I've written, because now I've forgotten it myself. It's the cocaine.

If only you were to come in the door right now.

If you were to come in the door right now, then we would forget everything, together. I would say to you, 'Come and stand over here, close to me, by the window, and let's look together through the glass.' Come and look at this beautiful night, the city flung wide beneath its lights, sprawling in a drowsy mass. Come closer and let your shoulder touch mine, as if we are children, little girls, sisters peeping out at the night in secret, concealed from their family. Tell me what you see. Don't let the misgivings whispering in your head get to you. You won't see anything but this night; there's nothing behind or above or beneath it. This is all there is.

Take off your shoes, let those pretty feet of yours get some rest. Don't worry about the time. Take as much time as you want. I'll go on standing here. I won't get tired, and I won't make any sudden move that might wake you up if you happen to lean on me and doze a little. I will remain here, standing here, even if I dissolve in place and my bones fall to pieces.

Wait. Wait just a little. I'll be back, I'm coming right back to you.

This man across from my window is watching me. He's been watching me for a while now.

He's not just someone who looks like the man with the heavy moustache. It's the man himself! He's from the secret police. This has nothing to do with using cocaine or selling it. I am not a dealer. I'm not a user either, or rather, I'm not enough of one that they'd be watching me from a rented hotel room, for days now, maybe weeks. A type from the Mukhabarat alerted by the people who refused my passport renewal at the consulate. This is so funny. Such a laugh, and so terrifying, all at the same time. Maybe it's an opportunity. I can just explain the whole situation to him and we can come to an understanding, face to face.

I'll be back. I will come back to you.

I t's because drowsiness is always hovering, ready to pounce… Or let's just say it's sleep's tyranny. I've never been much good at waiting for anything without nodding off, but here, for some reason, I haven't had to work at resisting sleep. The doziness I can never normally shake from my head and limbs hasn't come over me here, even though in this room I can't find anything stimulating to keep me pleasantly occupied. All I can do is to go on taking stock of the room's contents, sizing up the furnishings one by one as if they have some significance, as if every object will yield a grand meaning. When a person has nothing to do, when you're just floating in a void, you can't help trying to attach meanings to the objects around you, to find some connection with them. As if I can retrieve some memory of them, as if I'm already familiar with them, like they have some sort of place in my life or tell a story I already know. I've told myself, for instance, that the knob on the wardrobe door looks like the one I remember seeing in my aunt's home, in the old flat, the one she left during the war.

I stare at the wardrobe's double doors, following the patterns of the wood grain until my eyes are watering. Then I shift my attention to the drawer in the little bedside table, indecisive about whether to open it or not. I already know what is inside: a Bible, its pages thin and delicate, like you find in every hotel room in Europe, and an old telephone directory that no one uses any longer, and hasn't for a long time. The hotel cleaners must have forgotten about it.

How many of those who've stayed in this room have spent as much time as I have contemplating every one of its objects? Apart from whoever it was who left the letter inserted between the pages of the hotel directory. And that directory is surely not something most guests would open. In the first place, there's no need for a directory in a hotel as small as this. No need for it in any hotel, in fact, now that people have smartphones. It must be the owners' attempt at giving their hotel a veneer of luxury, a touch of the dignity of age. The directory looks old, its pages slightly crumpled and eaten away. Neglected and forgotten here, like the Bible.

The letter I found inside the hotel directory perplexed me. It worried me, actually. It talks about a young man, the letter writer himself. He wrote it in a cheaply rented furnished room in a street nearby, a rather run-down one, it seems. So how did the letter get here? Plus, it comes to an abrupt stop: it doesn't really end. All in all, because of this letter, I'm feeling very uneasy about the writer. It's not hard to imagine that he's in prison, for instance. The letter has it that he was full of terrible imaginings about the secret police from his country of origin mounting surveillance on him. So it looks like he went to talk to their man, and it must have ended very badly, and that's why he couldn't finish his letter. The letter is written to the woman he loves but she… I'm convinced that it was this woman who hid the letter, to prevent anyone who might have been looking into his activities from coming across it. Because, among other things, this writer confessed that he was living in this city illegally, and that he was taking drugs – things that could get him in trouble with the law. That woman might be why the letter landed in this hotel room, though I can't fathom how it happened, not exactly. And then probably she forgot about it, or maybe she hid it and then couldn't recall where she had put it. Whatever happened, the man never did return to the letter he had started. This might mean that his meeting with the man from the secret police – or the man he imagined was from the secret police – ended in some calamity. Maybe even a tragedy.

It's possible, instead, that it was the man from the secret police who took this room, in order to carry out surveillance on the young man who wrote the letter. And it was he who found the letter – that is, if he went to the fellow's flat searching for documents or papers – but then he forgot and left it behind here, perhaps because, in the end, it wasn't of much interest to him.

It's all this empty time, nothing to do. Idleness, the master of silly imaginings, stoking the explanations one comes up with for things.

Reading that letter, though, I could almost hear his voice. I could almost see that lonely, miserable, wounded man standing at his window, looking out at the emptiness of the night, alone without her – I mean, without that woman he loves, or who he won't...

The letter sounded like a goodbye letter, it really did. But who knows if he ever meant to send it, since he didn't finish writing it.

I'm more inclined to think it was the man from the secret police who got hold of the letter and hid it here, but then misplaced or forgot it. I mean right here in this hotel room, which does in fact overlook an area that must have a pretty bad name – all these dilapidated buildings bulging with furnished flats.

Why am I telling you all this? To entertain myself a little while I'm waiting, and also because the loneliness of that man, the letter writer, sounds a lot like my loneliness. Even if his story doesn't resemble my life in any way. But I sensed, I felt, his cry of pain as though I were an old friend, or as though I myself was the woman to whom he was complaining. Maybe I felt that way because after reading his letter, there were things I thought about telling him, things I wished I could say to him, and because I wanted so much to wrap my arms around him.

This is so strange. Especially because I didn't like her at all, that woman. If I were ever to meet her – which is a ridiculous thought, of course – I would give her a piece of my mind. I can even see myself accusing her of stealing the letter and concealing it here, so that it would be inaccessible to anyone searching her home, since possibly it was she who killed the letter writer and not the man from the secret police.

Or maybe it was her husband. Hmmm. He discovered their relationship and sent a hired killer. The murdered man believed this fellow was an agent of the secret police from his own country.

Yes, true enough, I'm hopeless. I'm always like this, swinging easily between my fertile imagination – the fantasies I construct, that is – and the reality of things, without giving much thought to what I'm doing. I'm always mixing up what happens in my head with what happens in the real world, but that doesn't worry me particularly. Actually, it keeps me amused. It's like having a dream at night and then being completely immersed in the details of it for the whole of the next day, and maybe longer. A friend who died some time ago might return to me in a dream, and then for days his presence goes on comforting me. It's not that I'm getting mixed up about whether he's alive or dead. I mean, I haven't forgotten that he did die. It's just that he seems to be with me, and that gives me comfort even though I'm well aware that 'comfort' might not be the most appropriate thing to feel, since the situation really calls for feelings of loss and grief – after all, I do know perfectly well that he's dead. It's as if he has come to visit me because I missed him, or perhaps because he was missing me. He comes to visit me, but free now of the things that were so painful to me before, the images

I had of each stage of decomposition as his body lay in the grave – swelling flesh, worms laying eggs, things like that.

But…what could be prompting me to write in this way? Such thoughts might scare you off, or convince you that I'm a bit 'fragile', a bit feeble-minded, perhaps. I think it's the letter that man wrote. I think it's the letter – that's what has tugged at me, made me spin these tales that are so… Yes.

It's just that I started writing to you as a way to fill up the time while I'm waiting. I don't have any idea what people find to do when they have to wait.

What I would have told you, if you were here, is this: I am not someone who waits. I mean, never, not even at the dentist's. Or what I mean is, when I've got to wait, I go to sleep. I have a really good nap. I wasn't like this before. If someone was late for an appointment we'd made, I would have no patience at all. I would be on edge, livid in fact, and I would stack up all the angry rebukes I could think of in my head. For a while now, though, I've been forgetting who it is I'm waiting for, and why I am waiting for whoever it is I am waiting for, and then my eyelids start feeling heavy. If I am waiting in a café, my head drops between my shoulders and I slump down in the chair, spreading my bag across my lap like a little blanket, and I go to sleep. It's not deep slumber, not like the way one sleeps at night. It's more like retiring into a dark interior space where the day outside disappears completely, or like the soporific state one is in after drinking heavily.

Yes…once you're here, I will be as chatty as I can, trying to entertain you, and also because you will ask me whether I got bored waiting for you. You'll ask because you'll be feeling a bit rattled, and a little apologetic, about being late. 'It was the snowstorms,' you'll say. Because what words will you find to say, anyway, when you enter this room and you look at me, and then you see me, like this, just me, all alone? I'm a lot older now. I'm old and I'm not like I was. I mean, after all these years. What I would have been trying to think about, waiting for you, was what to say first. What to start with and how to say it.

Someone who is waiting knows something, even if only a very little, about the person or the thing they're waiting for. Thinking about that person or thing keeps them amused, or distracted. Now, it's not that I know nothing about you. It's just that what I do know isn't very much, and it's ancient, and my memories are hazy. And anyway, when I'm mulling over what I know, bringing you to mind, I can't disentangle my memories from my inventions. This puts me on edge; it's not a pleasant distraction at all. This might sound odd to you, but to be frank about it, I can only keep myself happily distracted when I'm *truly* alone. To the point that even when I'm leaving the house, before going out I put on some music I like, because then I feel like I'm lingering a bit longer at home, in my solitude. As I'm returning, I can hear the music from outside, and as I'm turning the key in the door, I can think to myself, 'There it is, the same music, my music.' And while I've been out, no one has come in and stirred up the air in there. And so, really, I was there all the time, alone, with nothing to disturb me.

Little by little, day after day, my solitude has become the height of luxury. I cherish it. To be alone in air that no one else is breathing. It's become so important that I react terribly if someone happens to touch me or brush against me or knock into anything of mine, unintentionally, in the street or on the bus or in the lift. It's as though a terrible electric charge goes through me; I shudder and jump as if I've been bitten by a snake, and it is all I can do not to cry out with pain and anger. For example, this is what happens when someone stumbles and then seizes hold of my arm to keep from falling. I'm always aware that it's insane to react as I do. So I take a

deep breath, I smile, and I accept their apologies mag-
nanimously, trying all the while to hide that I've broken
out in a sweat and my heart is pounding, and I'm sure
my colour has changed as well. There must be many
people who suffer as I do when other bodies touch them
or even come too close. Like me, those people behave
politely without showing any sign of aversion or disgust.
In restaurants, many people – and not just me – look for
the shadows of fingerprints on clean plates or glasses,
not because they are passionate about cleanliness but
to convince themselves that the table bears no traces
of anyone who sat there before.

Even so, the letter I found here, stuck inside the hotel
directory, did not give me the feeling that anyone else
was in the room with me, or that he had been here
before me. Hotel rooms are forever inhabited by those
who have passed through. Each new occupant enters
cautiously, apprehensively, as though expecting to find
certain traces of the last person who was here. But I
found this room completely empty of any stranger's presence. It was as if, as soon as my fingers even touched
the written page, I sensed that the man who had left it
here was someone familiar, a person I already knew.
Even though it was written in a language foreign to
this country, and it was complicated to read. There
were words I could barely make out, and I had to read

the whole thing several times. Not to mention his poor handwriting, letters curling into themselves like dead insects.

But why am I returning to that letter?

Probably I felt like telling you this because I had begun moving about in this room as he was doing in his room – his 'home'. So I went over to the window as if we were going to it together. He and I. Then I pushed aside the curtains so that we could look out at the rain. As I was doing this, I nearly even spoke to him out loud, but then I came to, and I thought, 'That's the last thing I need!' At least I haven't begun talking to ghosts yet. Maybe I just wanted my voice to block out the sound of the rain. There's been no break in this heavy rain since coming from the airport. The sound of it has filled my head with noise. Its relentless pounding must have melted the snow that covered the city before I arrived. Or, more likely, it didn't snow at all here and I was just confusing this place with Canada, where immense snowstorms have moved in. Or perhaps I invented the snow as I journeyed from the airport as a way to tell myself that you would not be coming after all, not from Canada, since any snowstorm there would keep aeroplanes on the ground.

This is what I've become now. As I've already told you, it makes me happy to find things getting blurred in my head, or, to put it more honestly, to find myself blurring things in my head. So in the confusion of things jostling around in my brain, I've agreed to meet you at a certain time on a certain day in a small hotel at this location. But at the same time, I tell myself over and over that you can't possibly come – even though I am really here, in this place, and I'm waiting. I believe this has something to do with the age I've reached. After all, I spent an awful lot of my life trying very hard to do things the way they were supposed to be done according to conventional ways of thinking. It was only after great fatigue and strain that I let go, no longer obliging myself to follow other people's logic. Ever since my periods stopped coming, or more precisely after my father's death, all at once I saw a fissure open in the wall of my soul. It's true that this chasm allowed an icy cold to blow in, but at the same time it freed me from staring only at the blind face of a wall that had gone up around me, without my knowing by whom or when it was erected. It was sudden, this discovery: I began to see how fast the waters were rising around me, how the world was seeping in, pouring in, and how I had almost drowned.

My father had been my armour, protecting every part of my body from the things that threatened me. He was a magic helmet over my head, keeping out the lethal, black thoughts that might otherwise creep in. But because of his protection, and because of my love for him, I was bound in chains. I gave in to this submerged state of mine, protected by my ironclad armour and, for good measure, a full-body diving suit as heavy as lead. I may have been drowning, but I was protected. I was sinking into bottomless depths, where nothing could kill me, and nothing could rescue me.

After my father's death, I became free to despise people as much as I pleased. Now I could vent my hatred for the men I had fallen for who never did deserve my love. It was as though I had emerged from a past where I glided along on the greased rails of happy security, safe in the railcar of naïve goodness, without exerting any will or desire on my part. It was just that I lost half my life for the sake of keeping someone's love when I no longer felt anything for that someone. But since then, I've wanted to erase those men completely from the pages of my history. From my life.

It was in this spirit, I suppose, that I read the letter. It was a desire to insert myself into the logic of a man I do not know. To seek another place, a different place. An egotistical logic, freed of shackles, liberated and unattached to the point of being dissolute. A logic that doesn't ask for the consent of others: of the moralists, of all those associations and institutions that come together around principles and laws and 'the right way of doing things'. Such a logic means having one's own measuring stick, assessing the balance of courage and feebleness, success and failure, so that in one way or another, frailty itself becomes a source of great strength. Imagine a woman tested daily, abused and worn down, emptied of her soul day by day. Like that woman who killed her husband with his own rifle after a marriage that had lasted decades. In court, she said she felt no remorse. She would be ready to kill him again, without the slightest hesitation or doubt. From that moment, she said, she felt a kind of power fill her heart, and it had raised her above the mundane world for the few years of life that remained to her.

Would you call this revenge? Treachery? Or is it recuperation of one's most basic and primary right? The right to breathe.

One who is liberated does not have to be strong, nor does the strong person have to be free, as it is in the history books or in those legendary tales of heroes who are always and uniformly steadfast, staunch, courageous and bold, borne on a wave of light that bestows sage leadership on everyone in the vicinity. My neighbour, who threw himself from the fifth floor after his son was killed in front of his eyes, what concern did he have with the people around him, with the *whos* and the *whats*, with the priest who afterwards stood over his grave, rebuking his corpse because, he said, 'Jesus doesn't love suicides'? But everyone knows about Jesus committing suicide – everyone except the priest. My neighbour was an elderly man, with many ailments, weak in body and mind. But he decided on freedom, flying off the fifth floor. I might tell you, if you come, how I decided on freedom before flying here. We'll see.

I'm remembering now that I turned off my mobile before leaving the house. I should have left it on until the plane took off. Maybe you tried to reach me, to tell me that you would be badly delayed, or that you had changed your mind and would not be coming. That seems plausible. Although it was you who searched for me, indeed who wore yourself out trying to find me, according to what you told me. Despite my having closed my Facebook account a long time ago, you found me there, somehow, I don't know through whom. I will ask you, if you come. A person can change his mind, of course. But how will I know if you have changed your mind? The fellow in reception hasn't informed me of any phone calls. Have the snowstorms cut off the lines of communication where you are? Maybe that's it. Phone lines are always getting cut where I'm from.

A little before midnight, I remembered that I had not eaten anything all day. When I called down, and before I could order any food, the receptionist answered – even though I hadn't repeated the question I had asked him earlier – that no one had phoned asking for me, or to say they weren't coming. No problem! I opened my door and called the lift. I thought I would go out to the nearest bar or restaurant, but suddenly I felt exhausted, just at the idea of pressing through the rain without an umbrella. I was suddenly so tired and lethargic, and drowsy, that I felt almost paralysed. I got undressed and sank into the warm bed, keeping my clothes close by in case you should suddenly appear. I dropped off almost immediately but I woke up less than an hour later, with my knees throbbing and pain shooting through my lower back. 'I'm not all right,' I thought. 'I think I may be about to come down with something, or I'm sick already. I must get back to sleep quickly. Because I would look very poorly if you…'

Waking up at dawn, I felt completely recovered. I asked for breakfast in my room and I ate everything on that large tray. I pulled back the heavy curtain. It was still raining.

Nothing to do, but in a good mood all the same.

If you were here, you would be watching this sparrow with me. He hops about below in the empty street, in the rain, as if the downpour hasn't soaked him. A little bird without a flock to follow or be part of. A lone sparrow in high spirits in a big city of which he sees nothing. Maybe he is so old that he no longer needs anyone, though a sparrow never looks to us like it's all grown up, let alone elderly. A little bird is always young and never ages, as far as we're concerned.

Strange, isn't it?

No one knows why it is impossible for us to think about a sparrow growing elderly, to the point where the infirmities of old age carry him off to a natural death, like any other living creature whose life runs its course. Perhaps it's because we have never seen an old sparrow, or one that does the sorts of things we do that show we are getting on in life. For example, the way we stop erasing the names, or the addresses and telephone numbers, from the pages of our diaries even though they're the names and addresses of friends who have died. We don't feel we need to erase them in order to create more room on the page. Instead, we leave new names and addresses on the little scraps of paper where they were first written, scattered here and there, not transferring them to the diary. We're not afraid that they might go missing. What I mean is, we no longer care if they go missing.

Another example. I went to buy a new mattress, hoping it would relieve me of my chronic back pain. Looking at a mattress, I told the keen, solicitous salesperson that I really did not wish to pay for one guaranteed to maintain its quality and form for the impressive number of years covered by the warranty, surely many more years than I would be alive. In other words, I was not interested in spending a huge sum of money on a bed that would still be in excellent condition long after my death. I would be lying on it dead, and it would probably still look brand new, my body as stiff as the fine-quality wood frame. As one says of wood, it would still be 'breathing' under my corpse. 'I hate this bed,' I said, 'and I'm not interested in buying it.' And I walked out of the showroom.

It would be like having someone crucify you, telling you as he did so that this cross was made of the highest quality wood or that he was using only the most dependably rust-free nails. Analogous things happen frequently in our daily lives but we are not always paying attention, or if we are aware of such things, we do not know how to handle them. It's like a man in love destroying the woman he loves deliberately and methodically – precisely because he loves her so much he can't stand it. In my case, for instance, it really began to pain me to hear a man promise he would love me 'forever'. Such words terrify me, because that man is leaving me no space to change my mind, or to change, full stop. It's like being sent to prison for life. What if I were to cease loving him 'forever'? What price will be settled on the beautiful durability of the nails with which his passion fixes me to a cross?

You and I, we would have laughed and laughed if I had told you the story of the mattress, or of the cross. That is because you're about the same age as me, or a few years older. And after all that laughter, we would remember (perhaps) the great quantities of medlar fruits we ate as we walked the streets, which we continued to eat in the car that took us from the big square in downtown Beirut, from Sahat al-Bourj, to the Jabal – I don't remember now exactly whereabouts in the heights it was – so that you could meet up with a friend of yours. When we got there, I began searching for a rubbish bin or a barrel where I could toss my carrier bag now that it was full of medlar pits. I don't remember anything about that little excursion except how sick and tired I got of looking for somewhere to deposit that bag of pits, which left my palms wet and sticky. No, that's not quite true – I also remember the succulence of the medlar, which would never again taste as sweet.

This sweetness has nothing to do with the act of remembering. It's not delicious and sweet because it is linked to the past, to the time of our youth, where nostalgia for that time gives everything we can't bring back a more beautiful sheen. Nothing in my childhood or my adolescence has ever prompted a longing for the past, a past that seems to me more like a prison than anything else. I am not here in this room in order to return to what was, nor to see you and thus see with you the charming young woman I was, or how lovely and robust the springtime was that year, there in my home country. That country is gone now, it is finished, toppled over and shattered like a huge glass vase, leaving only shards scattered across the ground. To attempt to bring any of this back would end only in tragedy. It could produce only a pure, unadulterated grief, an unbearable bitterness. And anyway, seeing you, at the age you are now, is precisely what will immobilize my imagination, preventing it from ever again playing games with the image of myself that I've kept in my head, and forcing me to see that image very clearly and accurately – indeed, turning it into something nearly like my mirror.

I don't put on my glasses when I'm standing in front of the mirror, before I wash my face or apply kohl. That is not because I'm afraid of what my image in the mirror would look like if I were to see it unadorned and unblurred, but because I know that I am much handsomer than that image is, vastly so, and that the precision with which it reflects the pores and wrinkles, the thin layers of loosely hanging skin below my chin, is all simply an illusion, an exaggeration of reality, a 'scientific assessment' that is unwarranted and unnecessary. For who would come close enough anyway to see those details! What could tempt a person to do that? What reason could anyone have to breathe into my face while peering intently at my skin and features? No one apart from the dentist, but the dentist looks only into one's mouth. In any case, wrinkles aren't an accurate guide to how old one is. Teeth are. When the teeth recede, a little, but enough so they can no longer give you the pleasure of biting into a medlar fruit as you sit in the back of a taxi, so that its juice runs down over your chin and drips onto your clothing… When the problem is no longer one of where to throw the medlar pits. At least, that's no longer the only problem.

In your last letter, you mentioned some shared memories. My brain struggled to return to that past, and when it got there I didn't find anything. I tried hard to imagine that puzzling house that apparently we visited together, which you said belonged to a relative of mine. I couldn't come up with anything. And why would I have taken you to one of my relatives, anyway? And then, why were we eating shwarma from a spit, standing in front of the butcher's shop, if there was a family home only a few metres away? What girl from the village would ever do that – something only foreign tourists like you would do? Are you the one who is inventing things? Or am I the one who is erasing things from memory? Are you getting me confused with another girl whom you met in that country and then forgot? What you've said about me doesn't sound like me at all.

Or does the engine that keeps memories turning work differently for men's minds than it does for women's? For example, I remember very clearly that moment you brought your head close to mine, when we were sitting on the ground under a tree. I thought you were going to kiss me, but you didn't. Was it because I didn't respond by bringing my mouth any closer to yours? Where I'm from, girls don't bring their mouths closer. Maybe they do that in Canada, and that's what confused you, so that you thought I simply wasn't open to a kiss like that. Maybe that's it. Even now, and however much the desire might overpower me, I don't believe I would dare to kiss a man in the open air. But this kiss – or the absence of it – is not a tale, or an incident, that we remember in common or have ever talked about.

All of this is why it will really be a disaster if you don't remember that excursion to the Jabal. The medlar outing. It will be a huge disappointment to discover that you don't remember it, because I won't be able to think of any other expeditions we made, or things we did together that turned out to be fun. Or even any that weren't much fun. I might not be able to dredge up any memories at all, of any sort. Then it will be up to you to tell me again what you remember, in greater detail this time, to help me out a little with inventing things to say. Because we will have to say something.

Whatever the circumstances, once one has got past the age of fifty this business of remembering becomes quite easy sometimes, but it is also pointless. The life you've led so far can come back to you with staggering clarity, an unending stream of memories flooding over you even if you've made no effort to summon any of it back. Things that are remote, completely forgotten, turn up as if of their own accord, as if there's something automatic about the process. Places, smells, people's faces, details that have no importance whatsoever. Such as what a neighbour said many years ago about the benefits of rubbing copper with lemon and ashes when you don't have any copper pans or basins anyway... That sort of thing. Anyway, what use are memories like this when, even if you have learned certain lessons from the past, it is already too late to apply that knowledge? It's all far behind you.

It's very strange how much I want to see you.

By the way, I rarely travel. The few countries I have been to all disappointed me. They were *true* disappointments. Not because my country is more attractive – especially at war, going up in flames – but rather because the promises made by the travel companies were all lies. They have no shame, the way they lie! Total cheek. They come up with images of places that don't exist, or they bang together scenes of places that do exist, in a montage, and then they Photoshop the montage into a single image. Besides that, I have no sense of direction. Almost immediately I lose my way, and then, once I'm lost and panicking, I can no longer find any of the landmarks I'd picked out in order to avoid getting lost. I can't even see well, and in my fright I feel like a blind person groping along. I don't dare ask anyone in the street how to get back to my hotel – that's assuming I can even speak so much as a word of the native language. I don't dare ask, because I am so certain that I must be just around the corner from the hotel – so close that it will stir up their suspicions if I ask. Or they will try to help me with gestures alone, by sketching out a mental map, and none of it will stick in my mind.

Despite all of this, I've travelled all this way to meet you. Yes, I've come here to see you as if I really miss you. And I do. A lot. How do you explain that? Longing arises from distance, a distance that has separated two individuals who lived happily together for a time, a period when they did things together and spent whole days that were full of the two of them, and only them; days that united them in a togetherness that was both sweet and bitter, for better and for worse. What was it between the two of us? And what remains of what was between us? And why might you come? What sort of misplaced longing for days gone by might propel you back to me? Can you tell me how many days they were? Myself, I don't remember.

Whenever your features come to mind I get a lump in my throat, and the image of your face, so close to mine, your eyes gazing into mine, squeezes my heart.

The face I'm thinking of, naturally, belongs to a very young man, a man young enough to be my son now. If we were characters in an Arabic-language film, sensations

like this would signal a hunch, an intuition, and then
as the story went on, it would turn out that I really was
that young man's mother, and she had lost him or been
torn violently from him by the Pasha – because, in these
films, there is always a tyrannical Pasha who dispos-
sesses mothers. And that mother – that is, me – would
be guided wholly and absolutely by her heart throughout
the entire long, tragic tale. It happens in life too. Why
not? I love these films which you know nothing about.
For I'm – no, rather *we* – we are…we are all sentimental
creatures. I believe that you know about the Egyptian
diva, Umm Kulthum, as far as I can remember, but you
don't know Abd al-Halim. Maybe I'll tell you about my
boundless love for Abd al-Halim, and how this passion for that beautiful young Egyptian singer led me to
ruin… No, I won't, because it is a very sad subject and
it depresses people. And we didn't come here for tragic
confessions. But, in short, this man – Abd al-Halim,
the handsome Egyptian singer – destroyed my life. Of
course, you'd probably think that a silly thing to say,
or just a stupid joke uttered by a woman keen to come
across as *original*.

No, no, we will stay on happy topics. Maybe we'll talk
about those lovely spring days when we first met. About
the streets and squares we strolled through, how we ate
medlar fruits, drank freshly pressed juice, and all the

rest. I hope you won't go on about your job or your family or your country, or what your life is like now. Because if you do I will die of boredom, and I won't be capable of hiding how disappointed I am, especially if you launch into questions about my job and my family and my country. That would be very disheartening! Fatal, even. What I mean is, it would bring our planned rendezvous to a sudden and dramatic end. Because probably the whole point of our meeting is precisely not to learn much of anything, and not to use words that carry any meaning. The point is just to have the kind of conversations that you hear between strangers: light, inconsequential, as quick to disappear as a feather in the breeze, no sooner lying stationary on the ground than picked up again, wafting upwards to circle overhead once more.

Forget about Abd al-Halim. We'll find a lot to say on subjects we do both know something about. In the first place, there's this music that plays constantly in the hotel corridors, and the lift, and the reception area, even in the en suite bathrooms. We know all about this music, you and me. They've chosen Chopin, a Romantic composer who will tickle the hearts of lovers who have their trysts here. They must be hoping this will motivate those lovers to extend their bookings. From Chopin, we might move on to cinema. You must have seen *The Pianist* by now, with its Ballade No. 1 (Opus 23). The

Nazi officer will let the musician live because beauty has some power to lance even a Nazi's heart. No, forget about that too. I expect way over in your region of the world, you have views about things we'd disagree on.

Any of the items in this room could furnish us with something to talk about. Any of it could launch a pleasant conversation. For example, you might pry open the little fridge in here, and then I would start telling you how, at night, I sit at home in the faint light of the fridge in my kitchen, and I eat whatever my hand falls on, in an agreeable state somewhere between sleep and wakefulness. My sense of pleasure floats free – it is unconnected with my hunger or my insomnia, and I don't feel any guilt about it. I feel secure and quiet and pleasantly lethargic. It's a primitive sort of stillness, like the sense of well-being animal cubs feel. Then, once my stomach and heart are both nicely full, I go back to bed. And you?

Or, if you go into the bathroom, I might ask you, for instance, whether you normally use shampoo like the kind they provide in little bottles here, made with herbal ingredients to preserve the oil secreted by the roots of the hair, so it doesn't dry up and lose its shine, and the ends don't split. Do you? Or perhaps by now your hair is receding, or maybe you've gone bald?

If I go on talking to myself like this, I really will begin to look mad.

Yet we do have to say something, you know. Especially in the first quarter of an hour, if only to make out that we aren't really so shocked by each other's appearance, by how much we've changed and how old we've become, that we can't say a word. So many years have come between who we are now and that long-ago spring. So many years that you won't need your glasses to see, for example, that I have shrunk slightly – if you still remember how tall I was – and that now I am a bit stooped, my shoulders slumping and rounding. It's the back pain caused by poor alignment in my upper spine and neck.

Since you never knew my father, you won't be able to see how much I've come to resemble him. Yes of course, my father was a man, true, but with age my body has come to look like his, maybe like the physique of men in general. Now, when I cough, I think I'm hearing him. My lips are slightly lopsided, pulling my face down a little on the left side, exactly like his. Even the way I lie in bed when I'm going to sleep, or the shape of my toes: all his. At my age, I can't help thinking how many female hormones I've lost and how I'm now at that crossroads where male characteristics start taking over, before we – men and women – come to look more and more like each other. And you? Don't you have breasts by now, or hints of them?

I will try to orchestrate things – if you do come – so that I'm not standing up when you enter the room. So that I'm sitting on the bed or on the chair where I am sitting now to write. I'll be in a far better position than you, because it will be your physique that's in plain view, and it will be you who is nervous about facing my stare. But we are not in a contest! We're not afraid of each other. I think perhaps this apprehension formed in me when I read the letter I found here. The letter's lovesick writer is still a young man, as far as I can tell, or at least he is younger than we are, you and me.

True, passion has nothing to do with age. Right. But I myself don't believe that. Of course it has something to do with age. If, say, I am in love and greatly attracted to you, in some sense at least, or if you are the same, enough to make you fly halfway around the world to come to me, enough to get you all the way to this room, that means that we, the two of us, are attracted to each other enough to go to bed together. But that will reveal things, details that will extinguish the 'flame' of this attraction, or this love, if that is what it is. We will quickly deduce that due to my back pain, lying beneath you I cannot bend my body enough so that you can penetrate. Or you yourself won't be flexible enough to find a solution to this intimate dilemma. And if we keep trying and it just leaves us frustrated and tired, I will tell you that really, honestly, I don't want it. I'll suggest that we do something else, something more enjoyable. But what?

It's an embarrassing proposition. Maybe you felt it before I did. That is, you confronted it before you boarded the plane, or even immediately after you made the reservation and bought the ticket and wrote to me with the details of your arrival time and airline and so forth. Speaking about reservations, I'm thinking now about changing my reservation and postponing my departure by two or three days, but not in order to give you more time, for I know you aren't coming, since you haven't sent me an email and you didn't try to reach me via the hotel phone number. I'll stay on a few days because I like this room so much, and because the rain hasn't stopped, and I don't want to go out in this torrent of water. I'll wait, so that I can walk around a bit and see this city. And because I have the time. And because this little sparrow has my attention, as he hops incessantly around the same little space. And now, whenever I'm standing at the window to follow his movements, he has begun looking in the direction of the hotel.

No. I won't stay here in order to watch a bird. I'll stay here because something tells me that the writer of the letter I found here is coming back. I asked the very nice man in reception to tell him I'm here. True, the letter looks a bit old, because the paper it is written on looks old. It doesn't offer any hints or clues that would help locate its writer. In spite of this, I am going to try. I might stumble across him here or somewhere in Paris. In one of the cafés where young Arab men gather when they don't have anywhere else to go. The young men who are fleeing from something. Surely that will not be very difficult. Anyway, whatever the case, I am not going home. It would be impossible to go home now! And then I have nothing to do anyway, no one to meet anywhere. And since you aren't going to come I will erase Canada from the list of places I was jotting down, the places with possibilities for

I will find him, or at least I'll find some trace of him in Paris. Then I'll know whether he returned to his country after the revolution they had there, once he got his passport back. People don't just disappear like grains of salt dissolving in warm water. And when I do meet up with him, I will

M y Dearest Mother,

I'm writing to you from the airport before they take me away, and before trying to go through security. They are watching everyone. Every move. Because they're afraid of terrorists, they have everything under surveillance, starting with the main terminal entrance. They're all over the place, patrolling every corner, these plain-clothes officers.

But I was ready for this. To them I'll look like I'm just waiting for an arriving passenger. I'm not carrying a bag and I've opened my jacket so they can see I'm not wearing an explosives belt.

My beloved mother, I don't know if this letter of mine will reach you. What I really don't know is how long I can stay here. How much time I have, I don't know. I bought a newspaper so it would look like I'm reading, and I glance at my watch every couple of minutes, and then I go over to the big electric boards where arrivals are announced, and then I come back to my seat. This way, anyone who is watching me will believe that the aeroplane carrying the traveller I'm waiting for is delayed, and they'll go away and leave me alone.

There aren't many things I can occupy myself with in this place between places, amid all the people hurrying in and hurrying out. No one stays long, not the people saying goodbye with a wave and then wheeling round quickly to leave, nor those here to meet someone from arrivals, who compare their watches with the times up on the board and turn their faces to the outside doors the moment they recognize their passenger coming towards them from the gates. I can amuse myself a bit by looking at the variety of people here, their features and their distinct racial types, and the different ways they have of saying goodbye to their relatives or loved ones, each according to their colour and place of origin and religion. From their appearances, I can guess how they will behave. I say to myself, 'This woman is Sudanese, and she will cry as soon as that teenager standing next to her – he looks a little sad and worried, it must be her son – as soon as he leaves her to head inside.' 'This plump young woman with the blonde hair and jerky movements who can't stay still, she will positively start jumping for joy when she's finally hugging the person she's waiting for.'

This doesn't mean I'm writing to you just so I look busy. No. I want to tell you what's been going on before you learn it from someone else. You'll believe me, Mother, as you always have. Well, no, not always. You haven't always believed me, but I don't have anyone else to confess to. You won't be able to defend me, I know that. No one can defend me. But if I write to you, then at least you'll know how dear you are to me, and that in these very difficult circumstances, I am thinking of you. That's the least I can do. Maybe it's the only way I have of trying to seek a pardon. Even if you won't pardon me, just as you never do. You have never shown me any mercy, ever since they came to get me, at the house, that first time. Before I went with them, as they were already beating me, I told you it was just a trivial hashish case, nothing big, and there was no reason for you to be scared. You didn't believe me. You didn't believe me and you spat in my face. Maybe you wanted to convince them that I was really a boy from good stock, someone who should have turned out a polite and well-trained young man because his family had raised him well, and if his family was spitting on him now, it was because they were good, upright citizens who believed and trusted the soldiers. That's why I'm telling you now that I didn't feel angry about your spitting at me. In fact, it's become my fondest memory, your spitting into my face, because what happened to me after that was

You will not believe what happened to me.

I ought to have listened to you. I should have bowed my head and been an obedient child no matter what. I don't know now whether all those beatings my father gave me (the leather belt, the cane) were of any use, or whether on the contrary all they did was add more rage to the anger building inside me. Not just *anger* plain and simple. It was a sense of continuous blind humiliation, and to this day I can't see any justification for it. Even now my body aches from his beatings, and that is because I was small and innocent. I never, not ever, did anything to deserve that kind of beating. He always beat me in front of other people. He would drag me outside the house so that people would see that he was beating me. That he was teaching his son to obey. He might be a poor man but he was respectable and he took care of his family.

I know it is far too late for any words of reproof, even to you. Because I do blame you for never once protecting me from him. Why didn't you? Yes, he would have beaten you too, I know that. And it would have made him twice as angry as he already was, I know that too. But many mothers have stood up to a father, bending protectively over their boys and taking the blows that were meant for them. Many, but not you. All you did was to run water through my hair and over my face and say, over and over, 'He's right, he's got a point, he wants you to be a man. A man of good character – he wants to be proud of you.'

My father beat me because he felt like it and because he was convinced it was the right thing to do. It was as though he was preparing me for all the varieties of blows to come. God be praised! And with time, he did actually strengthen the resistance of my skin and bones, and reduce my sensitivity to pain. I got used to tightening my nerves against the pain I knew the beating would cause. And so, when I began going to the club, I already knew how important it was to prepare oneself in advance for pain. The club! We used to call it 'the club', even though there was nothing club-like about it except the dirt-filled sack that we competed with each other to punch with our half-bare knuckles. We wrapped them in bands of inner-tube rubber that the lieutenant fetched and cut for us. And this boxing was supposed to build on the upbringing we got at home, improve our moral fibre, push destructive thoughts out of our heads. It was meant to chase the images of women's bodies from our minds: those obscene pictures that led us to practise the secret act. Because if that ugly habit did not ruin our eyesight, it would drain the strength from our muscles, weaken our ability to fight and kill, and destroy our faith in the shining examples that we must all have before us.

Why am I returning to those days? Because I think I have a long time to spend here, I don't have any idea what is going to happen to me, and it's important to me to talk to you. Because you haven't seen me in years, and you don't know anything about my life since I left home, or since they made me leave home, that first time, and then the second time, when I dropped by quickly and didn't stay long, because

But I have to tell you that I got the whole idea to write this letter from a woman who was here.

She was a middle-aged woman, or maybe a bit past middle age. She was standing just over there, near the big sack of rubbish. She looked confused. I was just eyeing people, amusing myself, when I noticed her. She was looking around, and then she sat down and took some folded papers from her handbag. She opened them and began reading. After that, she sat there for about half an hour, just staring at nothing. Then suddenly she tore up the pages, dumped them into the rubbish bin and walked quickly inside towards the departure gates.

I waited a few moments before tossing my newspaper into the rubbish bin. And then it was easy to fish out the torn pieces of paper the woman had thrown in there, along with my newspaper – as if I had changed my mind. I mean, in case anyone was watching me. I only went back to my seat after I'd stood for a good while in front of the arrivals board. I've learned these little tactics through the kind of life I've had. Every scrap of knowledge we pick up turns out to be useful one way or another. But then I was startled to see that same woman returning to the rubbish bin and searching inside for the papers she had thrown away. I became more curious to find out what was in them when I saw how unhappy she looked about losing them. Unhappy, but even more than that, bewildered. Because the cleaners – she was looking everywhere, trying to spot them – hadn't come round emptying the bins. They were as full as they had been before.

Anyway. The thing is, there was nothing much in those pages. She had only torn them in half and so it wasn't hard to rematch them. There was nothing really important. Basically, she was just a woman who had been waiting for a loved one, or a former lover, but her hopes were disappointed because he didn't show. That's all, but somehow a light bulb flashed in my head and I decided it would be smart to hold on to the letter. In it she said she was going to follow another man to Paris, hoping to pick up his tracks there. But she's come to the wrong terminal, since none of the airlines in this part of the airport fly to Paris. It's a bit odd! And then, if there's nothing secret about what she is doing, why did she come back to look for those pieces of paper?

This woman said – or rather, she wrote – that it's impossible for her to return to her own country. These confessions of hers leave me suspecting that her home country is Lebanon. But there's also a big mystery about that. In this departures hall, there are no gates for airlines with flights to Beirut. I am very sure of that because I've read and reread the departure and arrival boards so many times. There's something going on, and that's why I decided that I might be able to make use of this letter in case they've been following me and they manage to find me here.

Never mind that. What I want to tell you now is that I have missed you, Mother, in spite of everything. It has been a very long time since we saw each other, so long that I doubt you would know me if you saw me. I have changed so much. I look very different now. I'm extremely thin, my teeth have fallen out, and I'm going bald. You would say that I deserve all this. You might even disown me, calling me the Devil's offspring. And if I think of my father, I'd have to admit that you have a point. Still, after all that I've been through, is there any point in believing that if I asked you to pardon me, you might do it?

I know you won't, I know there's really no hope.

At least you'll know that I am still alive if this letter reaches you. Alive, amid all the news of death that the sky rains down on us like pellets of hard-baked clay. I hope you're still alive too. I hope you got away in time, whatever route you took, by land or by sea. In the end, that's why I'm writing this letter, even though I don't even have an address to send it to! If only my luck would hold out, I would carry it with me and I would search for you. If I thought I could find you, I would put it in your hands myself. Because it is so hard to speak. To find the right words. It would be especially hard if I felt compelled to spill my whole story from beginning to end (as they say). If Fate rules that I have to pay the price for what I've done with my own hands, then you'll be the one who decides finally whether I am pardoned or punished. It's you who will be either my guardian angel or my executioner. Giving a pardon doesn't mean forgetting or erasing what's been done. Granting a pardon just means having some pity for a lost son who never understood how he could have been so battered by storm winds that he came to be what he is.

My beloved mother, I have changed a lot. I'm no longer the son you knew. I'm sick now, sick in my body and sick in my soul. And there's no hope that I'll get any better. All I can dream of is an escape that keeps me from dying in prison. That's what I dream of: an escape that lets me die in the open air, flickering like a candle before my flame goes out in some empty stretch of space, somewhere in God's vast desert. The Devil will receive my soul, my sick soul, and the Devil can do as he likes with it.

No one told me why the soldiers came and took me from the house. The first thing they did was to beat me: no questions asked, no investigation, no formal charges. They beat me and left me on the ground, then dragged me to a little room, returning to drag me out and begin beating me again. After that they put me in a van and moved me to a cell. 'Your friends confessed,' they said. 'We've got lots of evidence from the boys at the club who know you.' 'Fine,' I said. 'As talking seems to be allowed now, can I ask what I'm accused of? What did my friends tell you about me?' They just thought I was being cheeky with them.

Weeks passed, and then months. Their methods varied. I don't have the time or the space to tell you the details, but I can say that they broke me. They pissed on me and relieved their bowels over me too. When I was already swimming in my own piss and shit, they came lugging buckets from the toilets to pour over me. The pain didn't affect me any more, but the fear inside me made the 'rest' periods when they left me alone pure torture. It wasn't a fear of death. Hell couldn't have been any more brutal than this. It was a fear coming from somewhere I didn't know, and it always came over me when I was alone. Eventually, I came to prefer being with them. Listening to one of them telling jokes, for instance, I could tell myself, 'He's still a human being, he has a family, maybe he has children...' and I would start repeating that I was innocent.

But that fear, that terrible horror, devoured me, pulling me down into a pitch-black abyss and leading me to the brink of madness when they began to rape me. It only became unbearably painful once they started using glass bottles and clubs. It was a fear that grew by leaps and bounds when these rapes seemed to be happening in my dreams too. And then maybe only in my dreams, like my recurring nightmares about shit and all the useless attempts I made to get rid of it. To escape the stinking filth. I mean, I didn't have to be in prison to have these dreams. I could be anywhere, and before long I couldn't tell the difference between night and day, between what was really happening in my life and my nightmares.

Terror.

'I want to confess,' I said to them. 'I did lie to you, and I did all the things you've accused me of doing.' 'You have to prove you're telling the truth,' they said. 'How do we know that you've really repented?' 'I'll prove it,' I said. 'Work with us,' they said. 'Do whatever we order you to do. We'll be watching you, and so we'll know.'

I took it further than they expected. It wasn't easy to convince them that I had really and truly become their servant. They were wary, and they were constantly setting traps for me. But I succeeded, I passed all the tests. I wasn't lying to them, after all, and I had nothing to hide from them. The only thing I cared about was not being sent back there.

Little by little, I began to enjoy my new strength and power. I relished the deliciousness of my strange and startling transformation, the knowledge that now *I* had become the man who could strike terror into people – me! They grovelled at my feet like rats singed by lightning and called me 'sir'. You saw me then, in that blessed period, when I was back at home, having become a man – a man in every sense of the word, one whose father could take pride in him. A man whose father no longer needed to discipline him or teach him anything, since it was obvious that the state had taken that task over from him and had seen it through. So much so that… I'm sure you remember when he threw me out of the house. People had complained to him about me. 'Your son, may God protect him, is the one who tortures our sons after they're kidnapped. We just want them back. None of us is asking for anything more than that. We understand that they must have deserved what he did to them. All we want is to know where they are, and whether they are still alive. Could he please have them returned to us, now that he has seen to their rightful punishment?'

My father believed them immediately. He didn't ask me about it. He just snarled, 'Get out of my house and don't you dare ever come back.' When he raised his hand to slap me, I grabbed his arm, meaning to snap it in half. Instead, I spat into his face and walked out. I didn't feel the slightest sympathy for him. He was pushing me away, back to the place where I'd become this person, so that I would stay there for good, and I knew it was somewhere I'd be exempt from having to ask myself any hard questions, happy enough in my lower world, my shadow world.

My world – this underworld of mine. It kept me safe, like a giant warm womb, preserving me, the orphan without family. My only regret was that I didn't have more of an education, because then I could have gone for all the promotions. But I was satisfied enough. Anyway, given what or where I was, or what I had become, it wasn't possible to pull out or take a position of neutrality. So why should I punish myself with thoughts of remorse? Anyway, who was I to claim that these people were corrupt, immoral and murderous? And would I prefer returning to the hell I'd been in before? I loved being alive, and I wasn't the only one who was staying alive through such means. There were more of us than there are grains of sand in the desert. I wasn't in on all the secrets, and I didn't have all the information they had gathered. It made more sense simply to believe in what my masters and chiefs said and what they told us to do.

Were all these people thieves and sadists? No, certainly not. And some of them were my friends. We ate together, drank together, told jokes, enjoyed ourselves. Sometimes we exchanged tips based on our experiences conducting investigations. We weren't the political experts. Those people had their skills and their experience, their apparatuses, their files. They were the source of our information. In any case, we didn't trust those we interrogated, those who despised our country and our leader, and so, of course, despised us too. The truth is, our long practice in torture meant we knew exactly what would happen to us if we were to show any sympathy to anyone: that is, to put ourselves in their place. That old fear of mine had killed off any pity I might've felt for anyone. The only way to be safe was to be hard. It was much better not to try looking for the truth by listening to those we detained. Anyway, people who are locked up always lie, trying to save their skin.

There was no point in thinking about it, or in hesitating. Even when perhaps we went further than was demanded of us. That happened to me when I was beating one of those operatives who fancied himself a philosopher. The club flew, missed his back and hit his head and... May your life be long! The head of our operation said, 'Give him a number and take him away. Get rid of him somewhere away from here.'

All this made me understand, in some kind of final and absolute sense, that God is absent from this lower world, and that God left it to us to run things. So this must all be God's wisdom. I am a believer. It was God who gave me this mighty strength, because it is God who has planned and designed everything from the very beginning, even if our tiny brains cannot comprehend the greatness of His ends. That's why I was ready to obey my superiors. And since sometimes obedience isn't enough, I was one of those who commit perfectly executed atrocities on their own initiative, even before any orders are received.

I didn't want anything more than that, though of course I would have preferred to be able to send you more money. I know that was what I was thinking, but time defeated me. I still had a few stolen goods in my pocket – I hadn't sold them yet – when the world turned upside down. The big bosses disappeared all at once and the people invaded our headquarters and attacked us. The demonstrations mounted by debauched atheists and the dirty mobs turned into rivers of human bodies. I still don't know how I managed to slip out of their hands, which were pounding me from every side, hands and canes and stones. I fled.

I fled without a moment's thought. I spent long days and nights wandering aimlessly, covered in blood. In a neighbourhood on the edge of the city, a woman took me down to the river and washed me. She asked me if I was one of the men who had escaped from the prisons, and I said I was. When her sons returned home I started telling them I'd been in prison but had no idea what the location of that prison was. They'd taken me there blindfolded, I said. I talked about how they tortured me. I gave her sons all the details I knew so well. That was how I found myself in the opposition. From one opposition to another, I discovered there are many ways to get yourself somewhere else. I told myself, whatever it costs, whatever the dangers, I will travel, I will move on. In whatever country among God's countries it is, I will find some security. I'll begin a new life.

My beloved mother, I began a new life here, I really did. I learned what I had to of the language they speak here, in a short time. Then I entered the endless tunnel that is the process of getting papers. All the money I had was gone, after I'd paid a big sum to the smuggler who put us on a ship, and then more to the smuggler who set us on the overland route. We were on our feet for weeks. I followed the advice of everyone – individuals, organizations – who had anything to do with this process. In the last appointment I ever had with anybody from an aid centre or asylum seekers' bureau, the caseworker took out a thin dossier from her desk drawer and opened it. 'Someone from your country has testified against you. He says he knew you in the camp, he watched you, and you were working with the secret police. He says you personally supervised his torture in a cellar at one of their prisons.' I denied it all, with very strong words. 'Fine,' said the woman. 'But we will need to investigate.'

I never went back. I didn't go back to the refugee camp either. I was afraid of people who might recognize me. I slept in the streets with the Afghans and the Ethiopians. The Red Cross and some Islamic types brought us food and blankets. But then they kicked me out because of the alcohol. I had to join the huddled drunks with bottles clutched in their fists. I didn't last long among them. On one particularly cold day, they beat me and took my winter jacket.

Now I'm thinking about coming back. I mean, at this moment if the police arrest me, the only choice they would give me is to go back to my native country, if they give me any choice at all. Because they *would* like to get rid of us. I could buy a plane ticket and take a chance on getting inside. Once I'm inside the borders, I can look for a way to escape again. I'd have to find someone quickly who could get me forged papers. No matter what, I can't stay here, not in this country and not in the airport. Although for now it seems I've still got the space to keep on writing to you.

It was a cold and rainy day – the kind of drizzle that never stops and sends its dampness straight into your bones. I was trying to protect myself from it by pressing my back against the glass front of a supermarket, talking to a young man who was handing out free ad papers to anyone entering or leaving the store. In other words, he was a beggar. I couldn't help laughing when he began telling me his dreams of travelling to Hollywood, where he would definitely become a big actor, and then from there he would help me out…and so forth. I could tell from his accent that he was from Eastern Europe. I asked him where. 'Albania,' he said. 'Muslim, like you. I'd be willing to bet you're an Arab.' There was something about him I liked; or rather, I felt comfortable with him. Maybe it was because he was a beggar living off his own efforts. He wasn't trying to survive by informing on people or stealing and selling young girls.

A woman came out of the supermarket. She had yellow-ish hair and looked about sixty. She stopped, fishing for some change in her handbag to give to the Albanian. 'You're soaked,' she said to me. 'How can you manage in this cold? Where are you from?' I mumbled an answer. 'Aah, such a shame. I know your country, I love it. I have been there many times.' Et cetera, et cetera. When she saw that I wasn't inclined to chat about the magnificence and charm of my country, she changed course. 'Where do you sleep?' she asked us. 'There are places that take in people without...when it's this cold.' Putting the coins in his pocket, the Albanian said he slept at a friend's place, but anyway, he was going to emigrate. He was leaving for the United States soon. 'And you?' she asked me. When I turned my head away, not wanting to speak, she apologized for intruding on my business. She asked us if we wanted her to go back into the store and buy us anything. Anything except alcohol, she said to us, and then she wished us a good day and left.

She was back the next evening, with a very large carrier bag in her hand. She began talking about detestable egotism, and how one must think about other people... and so forth and so on, and that any human being is vulnerable to hard times, and how much likelier that is if he's having to suffer through wars and terror and leaving home...and on and on and on. Then she pulled a big puffy jacket from the bag and presented it to me with words of apology, hoping I would accept her modest gift. The Albanian had given me a thick woollen shawl. As soon as he saw the coat he came round the other side of me, undid the shawl from around my neck and said, 'C'mon, thank the lady.' I put on the coat and she seemed very happy. She began thanking me for having accepted her gift, which she called 'little', not waiting for me to come up with words of gratitude or acknowledge the favour.

I went down to the riverbank with the Albanian, to eat. He opened the carrier bag and began lining up its contents on the grass. I got into the habit of going to the river whenever I felt depressed or upset. I would stare into the moving water, and gradually I would settle down, and finally even fall into a pleasant state of drowsy stillness. I don't know why, back home, I never went to the riverbank near where we lived to calm myself. As if, once I was older, I had forgotten how I used to swim there with the other boys, how we would bob around in the only kind of bliss that we were ever allowed to have. We munched on wild grasses and sucked the eggs we found in nests. But later on, I never went, as if the water there was not real water. As if that had been another childhood, belonging to another man.

Then the Albanian started going on as if he were acting out a scene in one of his films. He said my mother must have made a vow for me on Laylat al-Qadr while celebrating the revelation of the first Qur'an verses to Muhammad. Or he said something like that, in his own manner of speaking. He said I ought to smile back at that woman who gave me the coat. I should humour her and be nice to her. At least I should answer her questions! He was fingering the hem of the coat. It was excellent quality, he added, an expensive brand only rich people wore. This woman must certainly be wealthy, he told me, and she probably lived alone, and he thought she was *taken with me*. 'I'll bet you she comes by again,' he said. He was an expert on women about her age, he said, women who lived alone and miserably, because their native countries weren't anything like our countries, where we took care of elderly ladies and respected the aged. I let him go on talking and we started joking around about old ladies' romances, and remembering how the Prophet Muhammad warned against falling for older women because it shortens your life. I even started mock-scolding him, saying that this woman he was talking of must be about the age of his mother. He stopped joking. 'God have mercy on her soul,' he said. 'We're not talking about mothers.'

When I stepped into her home, I was feeling convinced that God wanted to help me, and it was God who had sent this woman to me. He wanted to test my intentions about turning over a new page in my life. Her place wasn't a rich person's home, as the Albanian had imagined it. But, for me, warmth was the highest possible level of luxury, followed by a bed, any bed.

I had to forget my former life, the good and the bad. And I did forget it. When I sank into the tub filled with hot water, I didn't want to come out for anything, even a promise of Paradise. This providential woman, I would have kissed her hands. I did everything she asked. I helped her clean and tidy the flat, and wash and iron, and cook. Occasionally I surprised her by cooking one of our dishes.

Sometimes she asked me about my life. I always told her I didn't like to remember a past that had been so frightening, and I just wanted to forget all the pain and anguish I'd been through. After that, she started saying how much she wanted to help me get papers. And then, that she didn't understand why I refused. I told her I didn't want those documents. Then I asked her whether my staying there was risky for her. She said the law forbade her to take in foreign migrants, especially those without papers. She was a free woman, she said, and she did whatever she thought was the best thing to do. But because of this, she insisted that I not leave the flat, and that I must not open the door to anyone who knocked. Even the curtains – I had to leave them closed, and the lights out, whenever she wasn't home. This is what we had to do until we could find some solution.

When she was at work, I set the radio to the station that broadcasts in Arabic, which she showed me, or I watched TV if there was a boxing match, or a body-building programme, or football. It reminded me of the club. I would start trying to guess which of the guys there had told on me, or thinking back to things I'd said that they wouldn't have liked much. Then I repeated to myself that it was just jealousy. One of them must have envied my good body and the strength of the blows I could deliver, and so he invented some story to slander me. He claimed I insulted our president and leader, and that I was a communist or an Islamist and a member of the Brotherhood. It's possible that I let myself speak a little too grandly in front of those young men. Yes, because I was trying to keep distant the humiliation of the adolescent whose father beat him in front of people as if he was still a little boy. I'd begun claiming I had views and ideas, and that I knew a lot of things there that no one else knew, and so...

I could have become a famous boxer.

But I don't have any regrets about anything. To feel any remorse, I would have to know what it is I ought to be sorry about, but to this day, I don't know. I don't know what was in those pages of written confessions

99

and regrets that they forced us to sign with our own blood. And anyway, how can I think about 'regret' when I really didn't have any choices to make? Maybe I ought to regret showing off my strength so grandly to the men in the prison, or the lies I told to slander the sons of good families. But God understands that I was forced to do these things. God might remind me sternly that I got pleasure from the things I did, and that I was proud of them. This is true. If God questions me on these things, I will ask Him, 'What do You think led me to do that?' 'And You – why did You abandon me?' 'Why didn't You…?'

When the woman was not at home, sometimes I slid into a bad depression. 'My life has no meaning,' I would tell myself. 'This woman will throw me out soon, because everything ends sooner or later. And I won't be able to go on forever lying about my papers.'

I began opening cupboards and wardrobes and drawers when she was out of the house. From some papers of hers that I came across, I learned that she was in her mid-fifties. So she was quite a lot younger than she looked – probably due to the wrinkles across her face and hands. Even more likely, it was the moustache hairs that she apparently made no attempt to pluck out. She didn't pluck or shave anything, not her eyebrows or her underarms or her legs. By this time, she had begun to move around the house in front of me in thin, revealing garments, without any show of embarrassment. I would tell myself, 'She's at home, it's her way of being comfortable, free to do whatever she wants in her own place.' And I would remind myself, 'This is the way foreigners are. They aren't ashamed to show bare skin like we are.' I felt some shame and embarrassment, but she didn't.

Then she started telling me about the life she'd had with the man whose clothes still hung in the wardrobe. She told me how he had been unfaithful to her. He'd betrayed her, stolen her money and disappeared. One time I asked her – I wanted to show some interest in her story – why she still kept his clothes after everything he had done to her. She laughed and said she had lived the most beautiful days of her life with him, and she still loved him, and one day he would come back because no one else in the whole world would ever love him as she had loved him. Every so often, she said, she would air out his clothes and lay them in the sun, and wash and iron the white shirts, since otherwise, if they stayed shut away in the dark, they would go yellow. When I asked her how I would recognize him when he arrived, so that I would know it was all right to open the door, she said, 'You don't need to worry about it, he still has the key.'

From that day on I couldn't shake off a terrible sense of anxiety. But I didn't know how I could go on living with this awful feeling of uneasiness and fear. It became impossible for me to put on the jacket she had given me because I began to smell his odour in it. I no longer went anywhere near his clothes in the wardrobe. My heart would start pounding against my ribs whenever I heard the sound of footsteps on the stairs. But at least I did come up with a plan. If he were to return when she was out of the house, I thought, I would just say that I was a new tenant, and I didn't know anything about the woman who used to live in this flat. In fact, I would take the key from him.

I knew, then, that the blessed comfort I'd known in that place would not last. I knew that God wouldn't give me much more breathing space. That was just the way things were; there was no logical reason for it. After all, what good could result, or who would benefit, from punishing me? I began finding it intolerable to stay in the flat alone. By the end of the day, when the woman came home, I would be in such a high state of tension that I couldn't hide it. She thought my anxiety was because I didn't have papers, and so she would go on at me again, asking what it was I wanted to do, and why I refused to start the procedures, to submit the official request I would have to make in order to get those papers. This went on, until one evening she said she had learned about a new organization that could lessen the period of time one waited for acceptance – or rejection. This group could help me to replace the documents I had lost on the way, or that had been stolen from me by vagrants, which was what I had told her. Then she said, with a big smile that only accented her moustache hairs more, 'I told them about you.'

That's what did it. All of this anxiety inside me exploded into pure rage against the Lord and Master who had placed her in my path that day. I began cursing and shouting in Arabic, while she went on smiling, her expression ever sympathetic but tinged with reproach. And then, sometime during the night, I had an idea. I must make her fall in love with me so that she would not think about throwing me out. So that she would become attached to my presence in her home. Love is stronger than sympathy, after all. And so she would also stop waiting for that fraud who'd been her lover. So that even if that crook tried to return in order to steal from her again, she'd have put the thought of him out of her head already, and she would keep me instead, you see.

I woke her up. I told her that, first of all, I must apologize to her, and second, that I wanted to reveal and confess the true motive behind my anger. I began acting as though I were very embarrassed, and I started explaining to her that, in spite of myself, I had fallen in love with her. And that when she told me that she was still taken with the man whose clothes she kept in the wardrobe waiting for his return, I realized how strongly I was attached to her, and how jealous I was. Me, whom she had rescued, picked up from the street, whom she had been so kind to, saving me from dying of hunger and the cold; my feelings, desperately hopeless, had made me very ashamed. If I revealed them to her, I'd thought, it would look too much like I was exploiting her big heart, and this was morally unacceptable. 'Especially for us,' I said. 'We Arabs,' I added, nearly in tears by now.

It was a terrible night. She raped me, that woman, openly and ferociously. As I tried to fend her off, detaching myself even a little from her in hopes that she would return to her senses, she just clutched me more fiercely and attacked me again, like a wild animal. She had fallen for my play-acting. She wanted to rid me of the embarrassment and shame she'd heard me express. That's what she said. She threw herself on me, and began saying how insanely she wanted me, and how long she had felt it, and that I had made her forget the man whose clothes she was going to put out in the street the very next morning. That she was very happy I'd been so frank with her because she had been waiting anxiously for this but hadn't seen any signs of attraction or desire, let alone passion, from me. She said all this, on and on, as she undid the buttons on my shirt and yanked off my underclothes to take my member in her mouth and cup it in her hands.

Oh God. Oh God, what have I got myself into? That's all I could think. What daily hell have I cast myself into, walking into the flames on my own two legs?! The more I tried to refuse, the more it aroused her and excited her passions, and then the more I felt an overpowering disgust. I loathed her body, everything about her body, that pale, wrinkled, saggy old body. Her benevolent smile, her moustache-smile, her seductive little gestures that a girl of twenty would be mortified to try, the bright-coloured underwear she bought specially because of me, her springy step as she tried to sway like 'an Easterner' to Egyptian dance music, her girly coquettishness and affected coyness, her gifts, her cooking, her candles… This woman who had become another woman made me think about killing myself. Almost, yes, killing myself.

I told her one day that what we were doing was forbidden where I came from. She said she would marry me as soon as I got my papers. So then she kept harping on about the papers. Why don't we get the procedures going to obtain the documents you have to have, and then

The nightmares were coming back.

I'm in a very pleasant, even splendid, place, well lit and spacious. It's a party or an occasion of some sort. I need to pee badly, or to empty my bowels. I start looking for the facilities, but when I open the door to the toilet, it's another vast space with many doors, like the white, door-lined corridors of hospitals. I find a cubicle where I can do my business, except that the door to it is suddenly hanging off its hinges and the toilet bowl is overflowing with someone else's excrement. I try another cubicle but it's even filthier. Little by little, everything my hand touches, from the light switch to the wall I lean against, or anything I get tangled up in or bump into, or whatever brushes against my clothes, is dirty and stained with shit, and meanwhile I'm still searching; there are so many cubicles, one after the next, and so many narrow, cramped corridors I have to pass through, and they are also soiled with excrement, and I am still trying to find a little nook away from the gaze of the men and women who are caught in there like me. I am only trying to find a spot where I can relieve myself from the pressure of my bowels.

I'd wake up, pull off the covers and turn on the bedside-table lamp. I'd search among the bedclothes for those wet, sticky spots. I'd pull off my nightclothes and inspect them closely. I'd soap my hands over and over and call on the angels for help. I'd make a glass of tea and stand behind the window, staring out at the night. I would stand there a long time, gazing hard into the blackness, which was like the waters of a vast river, and I'd watch the running, gushing ink-waters until my breathing grew quiet. I wouldn't get to sleep again unless I cried away my torment, cried to the point of utter exhaustion and anger. If the woman woke up (she usually slept heavily), I'd shove her away, and she'd mumble, 'You're remembering the war, I will make you forget all your pain.' She would go back to her snoring, her conscience at rest, the conscience of innocent people, of the good and the well meaning.

Every morning, I began to feign sleep until she had left the flat. In the evening, she would find me bent over my writing, my pen scratching out any old thing in Arabic as I forbade her to touch me because I was working on a book about the war. The book became my great excuse. For here I was, completely preoccupied with thoughts and memories and all of the horrific secrets I knew. They paralysed me, those violent scenes that I could not keep out of my mind. They made it impossible for me to have sex, indeed they took me far away from the world of desire. Any desire. That's what I said, over and over, to keep her away from me.

This more-or-less tolerable situation did not last long. She began saying (again and again) that while it was all very well and good to write, talking was the true cure, the only real cure, prescribed by trauma psychologists as the treatment for victims of shock and the aftermaths of disaster. I must speak, I must expose the secrets, I must talk and talk to rid myself of the torments I had suffered. I must reveal what was in my deepest self, I must name the pain and the anxiety if I was to find relief and inner peace. That's what the woman with the moustache said, over and over, and then she proclaimed that it was love – only love and nothing else – that cured all illnesses, in more or less the same way that saints' miracles always worked. And she would love me without bounds. Love. Oh God.

I slipped out of the flat and went to find the Albanian. I gave him a brief version of what had happened to me, living with this woman, this old, ugly, horrible woman. He just laughed and accused me of being ungrateful, of forgetting those nights of chill and hunger and home-lessness and the bruises from beatings. My body had been eaten away by lice and scabies, he said, so who was I to refuse anything? 'Close your eyes and fuck her,' he said. 'Just work your imagination a little, your wet dreams, scenes from porn films. You're rejecting the blessings you've been given. Weigh it all up in your head, man. And then do what you want to do. Right, there's my advice.'

I went to see him a second time. 'Come back with me,' I said. 'Let's rob her. I know the place, I know where everything is, where stuff is hidden. She never locks any drawers. Money, jewellery, gold.' 'Why?' he asked me. 'You've got everything you need, as far as I can tell. Or do you just want her to suffer, as a kind of revenge? Anyway, revenge for what? You're mad, how would this help you? And of course she'll know it was you who robbed her, or at least that you had to be an accomplice since you're in the flat all the time. And then, why would I put myself in such a risky situation when I'm waiting for my asylum papers? You're mad. Leave me alone. Don't come back. I don't want to see you here ever again.'

I bought a bottle of whiskey and I went back to the flat. I began gulping it down as if I were a parched wayfarer who'd suddenly found a spring. In the evening she yelled at me like you'd yell at a little boy, because I had gone out of the house and because I was getting drunk. She snatched the bottle of whiskey from me and poured what was left down the sink. 'What will you do next?' she whined. 'Look at your gut, getting fatter and fatter. Instead of exercising you're just falling back on alcohol. I'm not putting up with this!' I was afraid she would throw me out, so I tried to humour her with a little dancing, to show her I could still move gracefully, and to make her laugh.

'This woman just doesn't know who I am,' I began repeating to myself. 'She doesn't have a clue, and she doesn't understand me.' Seeing that she had no fear of me, I became convinced that I was diminished. I no longer had the power to frighten others. At least I still had control over my anger; I could swallow it when I wanted to. But when my own fear came back to me, I couldn't control that. It came on suddenly, like a heart attack or an epileptic seizure. It made my eyes fog over and my whole body go numb. Suddenly I was back inside my old nightmares, but this time that fear was locked arm in arm with the dread I'd injected into the eyes of all the people I had tortured. As if I was collecting this enormous double portion of fear inside my own head and body: the fear I'd had of those who tortured me, and the fear of those I tortured. All of that terror accumulating in one enormous ball that went on picking up everything in its path, one mass growing bigger in its fear, swelling to a giant size in its pain.

And the woman, this foreigner with the moustache, poured her tender care and her passion over me. She embraced my worries about the book. She called me in to watch the news because I needed to know the latest developments, she said. If I didn't watch, she summarized what was important in the news, significant to the revelations I would offer in this book I was writing. Once I had a book with my name on it as the author, the authorities would take a different view of me. In any number of ways, it would ease the way to getting the papers I needed.

My darling mother, evening is settling on the city. The glass walls of this outer hall in the terminal are like mirrors reflecting the lights, and no one has come anywhere near me. I see wet coats, so it has begun to rain. There are not as many people coming in and out, now that night is falling. I'm still thinking about buying a ticket to come back. I'll tell them I wasn't successful at getting a resident visa, and that I don't have any documents on me to prove who I am. They'll interrogate me for an hour or two, or maybe a bit longer, and then they'll chuck me onto the aeroplane.

Or I could tell them I'm an undercover detective. That I'm following the woman who tore up her letter and then got away before I was able to pick up her trail here and stop her. And I have this letter, here in my hand, here it is, and because I've studied whatever there is in her file, I know that she did not return to her own country, because... Well, I will say, because she killed her husband in order to meet up with this man she loved, or this man she was having an affair with, and then he would take her to Canada, and there she would disappear. But the lover didn't actually come, and so she changed her plans and has gone looking for refuge elsewhere, with another man. It's all there, the letter gives all the details; it's documented, and so they've got to allow me to follow her.

But since I don't have any papers, they won't believe me.

Or I could go back to the woman's house, have a look around at the way I left things, and see, for instance, whether her former lover might have turned up, using his own key. I need to go back there to change the lock. I forgot about doing that.

Or maybe it's better if I sleep here tonight. I won't find anywhere open now where I can buy a new lock and key, and I won't find anyone who would fit it after taking the old one out, not now. It's late.

I killed that woman. The work of an instant. In a moment of terror and panic that seized me and completely over-powered me, I killed her.

I was sleeping next to her. All of a sudden, she pressed herself against me, hard. I was half asleep but I had the sensation that worms were crawling over my skin. I even saw the worms. I pushed her hand off me, pushed and rubbed it off me as if I were scraping worms off a corpse. But she started touching me again and pressing herself against me, against my limbs, my organs, everywhere. My head erupted. Alarm, anger, a combination of the two. Poisoned blood shot blue-black through my body and clouded my eyes.

Now, because I'm recording what happened, I'm trying very hard to remember all the details in their order. This is not because I'm trying to find excuses for myself. After all, it so happens that I killed a lot of people long before I killed her. None of it affected me much: not their screams, not their blubbering and pleading, not the gurgling sounds as they died – hanged or strangled or buried alive in coffins and then shot at. Inside, they struggled and pounded and scratched as though they meant to wrestle the bullets from where they'd lodged in the wood, before they went quiet, giving in to their fate. Even the smell didn't bother me. It was just an outcome, as I saw it, of what was more or less a natural process, human flesh decomposing. I slept soundly, undisturbed by any regrets, feeling no alarm, no anger. Torture followed by death was going to be either my lot or theirs, a final decree that there was no escaping.

As for getting any pleasure out of those things I did, deeds God might well make me answer for? Well, what I did was simply the most natural path to follow: a person wakes up at dawn and goes back to doing whatever he was doing yesterday. It isn't a matter of choice or pleasure. Feeling pumped up by your own strength and audacity and the absolute power you have over people isn't just a nice little luxury you can take or leave. Seeing men who were once army officers, or university professors, or judges, kissing your feet and bawling is more than a mere treat you come to expect, to top off your day. It grows into something you have to have, without even being aware of it. Because when these things happen, the blood rises and boils in your heart, thickened and heated by natural intoxicants which mimic the drugs that create the addict's pleasure and bind him forever to those substances. When you can overturn people's lives and make them into different people, when you can recast their fates completely with your own two hands, you become Fate itself. Fate, to which you used to supplicate on hands and knees, desperate for it to be merciful to you. But this time around, that's not where I was! My interests lay in keeping her alive, that woman. She was my only refuge. It did me no good at all to kill her.

I wasn't really aware of what had happened until the next morning. She was lying there as stiff as a board, her arms outstretched and her legs splayed. Her hair looked like a bushy, tangled ball of thorns and her eyes were wide open and bulging. Her tongue was bluish and it hung from her slack jaws. So I must have strangled her. There were blue rings on her neck and beneath her buttocks a pool of cold urine. The fuzz from my nightclothes clung to her fingers and nails, and I had some trouble picking it out. I covered her face and then her whole body with the bedclothes. I went into the kitchen, made coffee and sat down on the stool. God, she's ugly, I was thinking. She really is hideous now. What's happened has happened; maybe it all happened because she's so disgusting, and now this disaster has landed on my head. I mean, she's dead now, so she won't be conscious of any of it. But I'm alive and I have to find a way out of this mess I've got myself into. Getting rid of the dead bodies was never part of my job. There were always others assigned to that and I didn't know anything about what they did.

My next thought was that I could just leave her as she was and run away. Immediately, and fast. But where to? Her Algerian neighbour who lived in the flat below was back from holiday. And the woman had always told me that she was the only person who ever visited this downstairs neighbour and chatted with her. That was because now and then, she – that is, the Algerian – came round with a platter of couscous or some other dish she had made. So, what if the Algerian woman came up here and knocked on the door one of these days, and then the next and the next, and it began to dawn on her that her neighbour was missing, and she got worried? I wrote out, on a slip of paper: *My dear neighbour, I'm away for a few days, and I'll see you when I am back.* I stuck the slip of paper on the door of the flat, closed it and returned to the kitchen. What if the Algerian woman noticed that the handwriting wasn't her neighbour's? But what evidence did I have anyway that the two women ever exchanged messages, and knew each other's handwriting?

I was in a real fix. I needed some time. That was all I needed now, I thought. This woman who enslaved me and poisoned my days was not going to be the end of me – this woman who had made me into one of her pet dogs, because she cared so much about strays.

I turned on the radio. It was her favourite singer, screeching out lyrics in a raspy, terrible voice. I'd heard that she began life as a whore in the streets of Paris. I turned the radio off. Forgiveness – it's a divine secret, who gets forgiveness. They forgave the whore. They made her into a big star instead. Who would forgive me? Where would that come from? Your heart? My mother's heart? Hahaha!

Do you remember that poem, 'A Mother's Heart'? Do you remember how you made me memorize it? How you kept saying this poet was a genius?

> A man once met a simple youth,
> Said, 'See here, lad, now here's the truth,
> If you do what I tell you to
> There's jewels and cash in it for you.
> Now fetch your mother's heart for me.'
> So he stabbed her, cut it free,
> But running, fell and dropped the heart.

And it goes on...

But just imagine, now, the child stumbling, and then the heart falls and rolls across the ground, and it is the heart that calls out in worry. 'My son, my darling, are you hurt?' And when the son realizes what he has done and begins to bathe his mother's heart in his own tears of regret, and then tries to knife his own heart in remorse over a lesson learned, his mother's heart comes back at him, screaming, 'No! Take your hand away! Do you want to kill my heart twice over?'

Hah. It's a tale that calls for laughter so strong and wild that it opens the lungs to their painful fullest, where they're siphoning off air like a running sewer pipe until it hurts so much you think you will burst. Sometimes one just has to laugh and laugh, to keep away the demons of depression.

Anyway, I still have this bad poem in my head. To this day. I don't understand why or exactly how the man bribed that boy. Or how people can teach children such terrible things: a bloody knife stab, slicing a chest open to draw out the heart, and then a heart stabbed to death that screams words as it falls and rolls. Ya latif altaf! Good Lord of ours, be kind to us! So, what this song really says is that a child *could* do something like this, even if for most children the possibility would just live in their imagination. And then, it's also saying that the child can be certain of his mother's forgiveness, without ever having to seek it, because she will forgive him no matter what, and in advance, and instinctively, even for such utterly primitive, barbaric behaviour, which also takes violence to the extreme. Or perhaps, that she would forgive him the violence of this most primitive of acts. Would she? Really?

It is, of course, the most extreme kind of violence, and primitive barbarity, to mutilate a body. *Your* heart, whether it is still in your chest or somewhere beyond, will not forgive me, even if I've had no choice about the things I have done. Shame, violation, the unthinkable! But I have given this a lot of thought. And I know what it means, but the circumstances we're put in have their own laws of necessity. I never in my life had to do any-thing like this, to mutilate a body. We assigned certain condemned men to carry the dead bodies out to the waiting lorries, and after that – I don't know anything. I don't know what they did with them. How could I have possibly hidden the body, even for a short time, just enough time to ensure I could get out of here? Where would I hide it? I thought about one of the wardrobes. Impossible. The body was too stiff.

My Lord will bring me to account. And I will ask Him what I could have done. 'What could I have possibly done differently, once You cast me into the furnace, into the furnace of Hell. What could I have done, once You rid yourself of me, Lord?'

119

I will go back there tomorrow to change the lock, and then immediately I'll come back here. God have mercy on her, and God help me.

I guess I will need to consider whether to keep this letter I've written, so that I can send it to you, or give it to you directly. Maybe instead I should destroy it, given the bare confessions it contains, which could well send me to the gallows or to life in prison. We'll see, tomorrow.

I'm going to add Fairuz to my phone playlist, and I'll go to sleep listening to her sing. I will try hard not to cry. Her voice is so beautiful. So tender.

My darling mother, wherever you are, sleep well. Good night.

M y Dear Brother,

I have been thinking about writing to you, now that you have learned what you call 'the truth'. You're right to call it that, up to a point. But the pure, unadulterated truth is something other than what you believe it to be. Everyone has secrets, and you must help me with a secret of mine, because it is in both our interests. I don't have much time.

We are waiting for a plane to land; it's still in the air because the plane at this gate that was supposed to make way for it was delayed. They pulled a passenger off that departing flight. The plane had already taken off but they made it turn around and come back to the airport. I know why security took him away in handcuffs, because I have a letter in my pocket that this man wrote to his mother. He must have tried to hide it before they reached him, because it's not the kind of letter anyone would just forget about or be careless enough to lose. I found it when I was putting the aircraft seats back in order after they unloaded all the bags and made the passengers disembark so they could search the plane. The pages were crumpled up in a wad and shoved down between the seat and the wall of the aircraft. When I saw it and could tell right off that it was written in Arabic, I stuffed it into my trouser pocket. I know now why they didn't search his seat very thoroughly. The man wasn't a terrorist, he didn't have any bags or weapons. Based on what I read, the guy is just a criminal. He killed a woman who'd given him a place to stay, and he needed to get away. So they know his crime. They'd already found the woman's body and were on to him. He tried to escape but couldn't manage it.

It's dreadful, what the man did. But because I delayed handing over this letter to the police, having hung on to it long enough to give it a thorough read, I can't very well give it to them now. What excuse would I have for keeping it this long? Anyway, since they've arrested him, they don't really need the letter, which would only add a few details to the charges they've already got against him. Plus, it's written to his mother. His poor, miserable mother; where she is now only God knows. It's a son's confession to his mother, the last person one can go to in life, the final resort – whatever it is he has done, and whatever she has done. I couldn't find it in my heart to give the police these final words he wrote. I was afraid, yes, but apart from that I felt real sympathy for him. That's bizarre, of course, because he's a criminal, a murderer. But every person alive in the world has an innocent side and it shows when they stand in front of their mother. In front of a mother, everyone becomes a little child again. The child-self left behind long ago, and all but forgotten. Later on, I will have to think about what to do with this letter.

Your mother's heart: it's the last, the final, heart you have in life. I lost my mother, just like this man, the letter writer, who will spend all the rest of his days in prison. At night, alone, he will weep for his mother. Far from everything he knows, estranged. He too is a person whom Time has abandoned, or Fate, perhaps. No one will have mercy on him, neither God nor any human being.

It's because she is our mother – for she is your mother too – that I'm writing to you. The truth is that I lost her long before she died.

I could never figure out what caused such a change in her. In a nutshell, all the money I was sending her was no longer enough. She would tell me that Umm So-and-So and Umm What's-Her-Name, the old bags (and they too were somebody or other's mothers), were rich by now. People were building houses and blocks of flats, and buying all sorts of things that cost hundreds of dollars. She couldn't stop talking about how the girl's expenses were going up and up. 'The girl's eating so much.' 'The girl makes so many demands. She has to have this, she has to have that.' I could only believe, in the end, that my mother no longer wanted my daughter there.

I phoned her. 'Mama,' I said, 'I love you. And you have put up with so much from me. As long as I live, I will never forget what you've done for me. Just give me a little more time, and I'll collect the girl and bring her to live with me.' But my words made her angry, and she began cursing me over the phone. She said her patience had run out. My sweet talk wasn't a solution. 'Do you want me to work the streets?' I asked her. She hung up on me. After that she no longer picked up when I rang her.

The pain and stress of it forced memories on me of how my mother had been behind my miserable marriage, which she forced on me before I turned fourteen. She never forgave me for insisting on a divorce, and you didn't either. In fact, the two of you were the reason I fled to this country. You are the reason I have worked here as a maid, cleaning houses and scrubbing the filth of people I don't know from restaurant toilets, hotel rooms and planes. Mother was contented enough in those days. I had gone away and that put some distance between her and the scandal of my divorce. And I sent money to her regularly, enough to take good care of all my daughter's needs. But those daughters of the women she knew, like So-and-So and What's-Her-Name, had 'broken protocol', as they say so politely here. I began hearing about how the girls were making trip after trip home. One of these girls would arrive with armfuls of gifts, pricey brands, showing off her jewellery to the many visitors. I was hearing about how she would hire a car, build a house, do things that allowed her father to stop working. No one seemed to be asking where all this money was coming from. When a girl is wearing a hijab, and often covering not only her hair but her face as well, how can anyone have doubts about her morals?

I couldn't get my mother's angry complaints out of my head. After all, hadn't she basically sold me off to that man who married me, for the price of the dowry he offered? That didn't furnish me with what a bride ought to have but it did furnish my family, easing the financial burden on all the men. I didn't see a penny of it, apart from the price of the ticket that meant I could vanish from her sight after my divorce. No, I didn't see a penny of it. I endured all that hardship and misery, hoping that she would come around, that she would understand me and treat my daughter well. Sixty lavatories I was cleaning before 10.00 a.m., running tens of kilometres in a race where the only hope of reward was a smile from my line manager – and she was a woman who never smiled. And what did I have to show for it? That's what I began asking myself.

I cried stinging tears over the way my life had gone, and then I decided to work as a prostitute. A whore. A streetwalker. What is the difference between one kind of humiliation and another? Only money, a little money, would lift me a notch above the stink of the lavatories and the filth of the depths I had sunk into. After all, it was my mother – my own mother! – who was the first to grind me down. You…well, you had gone to prison by then. I kept my part-time work as a hotel cleaner just to make ends meet.

It was easier sleeping with my customers than it had been having sex with my husband. They treated me gently, politely, spending half their time talking to me, and then flirting with me. They awakened me to a world of pleasures I had never tasted in the past, and on top of it, they paid very generously. My one condition was that they not take me from behind, like that pig did – by force, until I was bleeding. I think he preferred men and he was trying to hide his desires even from himself. I can see that now, having become a woman.

I had heard a lot about how much street women suffered, but I didn't see any of it. No pimp, no unsavoury houses. I selected my customers from 'Evenings in the Afternoon', that is, from the tea dances where older people gathered from mid-afternoon, following their dessert after their midday meals, until returning to their flats in the evening for soup before bed. Most were retired men. Some were married men, bored and restless with their lives at home. I only approached men who showed up there alone and those who were new regulars.

At first, they didn't understand what a young woman like me was doing there. I didn't much like people of my own generation, I always told them, and I was a romantic. I played the role of the innocent young woman, maybe a little naïve, maybe even a bit simple-minded. At their age, this was the type they preferred. And they could recognize the type by my clothes. I kept to old-fashioned styles they would have known from back then, when women really made them enjoy life – a style of dress that reminded them of their youth. I got some enjoyment out of it too, because they found me pretty. The low lighting inside, the reddish glow it gave out, could take ten years off a man's age, perhaps even a little more. That's why, emerging into the natural light, they usually hurried away very quickly. Even in the dimness of early evening, the outside light suddenly brought back all those harsh years they had lived. The light exposed the fatigue and sweat on their careworn faces, the make-up running down their cheeks and the thin hair plastered to their skulls. They always scuttled away, except when it came to me. With me, they lingered on the pavement. It didn't take long for them to realize what they had to do if they wanted to be alone with the flirty, flighty girl.

The men I singled out were the ones with soft hands, those who got their nails trimmed at the salon. That signalled a man's financial status to me more convincingly than the smartness of his clothes. I became expert too at judging the quality and cost of a man's shoes, and it wasn't about the age of those shoes or how much wear they had had. Those men were so delighted with me that I never felt embarrassed at taking the money they gave me, offering it as though it were a gift, albeit a modest one. In fact, in view of their loneliness, I truly felt I was doing each of them a service, giving him back confidence in the magic of his manhood. You would have to see how they thanked me to believe what I'm saying. With them I was a respected woman, a respectable one. I didn't have any doubts about that, and I was happy about it.

Everything was fine until I encountered that Arab man in the hotel. He came back to his room while I was still cleaning it. He began making a move on me, using offensive language. I answered him in Arabic, hoping that would make him suitably ashamed of himself. But he just got uglier and then he attacked me. He hit me hard, he beat me, and he raped me. I sent for the hotel security and the head of personnel. I showed them the bruises, the red marks – the signs of my beating – and my torn clothes. They took me down to the ground floor and when I went on screaming in the lobby, they said, 'We know you're a whore, but we've looked the other way. It's your life. But making up a scandal to extort money from this rich guy just because he's an Arab and he's afraid of scandal – no, we won't go along with that.' They threw me out.

That's how I moved to the work I do now at the airport. A gentleman, one of my former clients, put in a good word for me. I had set some money aside, so after the incident in the hotel, I decided to fetch my daughter and bring her to live with me, and of course to stop seeing any men.

My very dear brother, listen closely to what I have to tell you.

I went back there, my arms full of gifts, in a hijab, just like all the other women there. I went further – I wrapped my body in black from head to toe. I found our mother sick and bedridden, but my daughter wasn't there.

'Your daughter ran away,' my mother told me. 'I don't know where she is.'

Her neighbour, Umm Rashid, took me by the hand, led me to her home and sat me down. She told me that my mother had forced my daughter into marriage and now she was living in the Gulf with her husband.

Umm Rashid and I worked hard to find out what had happened. She knew the shaykh who had performed this marriage, which was forced on my underage daughter, and I eventually got the name of the man who'd taken her. From embassy to consulate to the family law judge I went, and finally I got an address. I travelled there and I found her. I found her working as a maid and a dancer in a house that was more like a brothel. He had married her, as he had dozens of others. When I met him, I was surprised to find he was neither a man nor a woman. He was some kind of trans, a man who dolled himself up, wore women's dresses and moved like a woman. He was an ageing man, grown fat with his dissolute behaviour. I felt my hair going white. 'My daughter is underage,' I said. 'I am going to send you to jail.' 'Take her,' he said with a wave of his pudgy hand, his fingers bulging around his fat rings. He ordered the people perched around him to haul us outside.

The whole way back to our home town, my daughter didn't say a word. She wouldn't answer any of my questions. I confronted my mother, asking why she had sold off the girl when I was sending her plenty of money. I knew from Umm Rashid that an odd-looking lawyer with very strange manners had been coming to see my mother regularly, about getting her son – you, that is – out of prison. He deceived her and took her money. My money, all of it. It was all mine.

I turned the house upside down. I found gold and silver there. I found the property deed to the house and I forged your signature and my mother's. I bribed the people I had to bribe and I sold it. Am I the one who removed her bracelets and pendants from her hands and neck as she lay on her deathbed? Yes, that was me. Did I leave her to die alone, not even summoning the doctor at the free clinic? Yes, true. But it is not true that I suffocated her with her own pillow, as you once hinted I'd done.

My daughter still would not speak even after I brought her back here with me. I told myself I would see her cured, even if it meant taking her to the very best clinics. You can probably imagine the rest of the story. Because of the girl I had to find more income, and so I took another job as a maid. The lady of the house couldn't stand me. I don't think she could stand any human being. The first time she slapped me, I stayed silent. When she wasn't there, I was using her toilet and not the servants' washroom. That's what she said to me. Nothing provokes hatred more than poverty. She took pleasure in humiliating people, even her husband. Maybe her husband more than anyone else, and to a point where sometimes I felt sorrier for him than I did for myself. He loathed her, too, and I served him well when I let that woman die.

Yes. I saw it, I saw what was going on when she fell in the bathroom, bleeding. 'She's fainted,' I said to myself, 'that's all.' I left her there. I stole all the little jewellery boxes she had and the chest that contained her really pricey gems. I stole some money that I found in a desk drawer in her husband's office. I left the place, closed the door and locked it with my key. It was I who alerted the police, saying I'd discovered her body after I returned to the flat, as if arriving there for the day. That's what I told them, that I'd arrived and found her body. They accused the husband, who had no money and no work, and who always complained to everyone about how bad-tempered she was and how difficult she was to live with. They declared he had faked the theft and murdered her in order to inherit. They threatened me too, and then they searched my home thoroughly, but they didn't find anything. They believed then that I was innocent. I cried really hard while they were interrogating me. It was an honest reaction; I cried because I was terrified, and I feared for my life. They thought I was crying because I'd been accused when I was innocent.

Brother, I did not kill my mother. I did not kill that woman, either. I left both of them knowing they might die, but that is not the same thing. In fact, they might have died even if I had made some effort to save them. I am not a murderer. This is the will of the Creator, it is His judgement. Why should I not accept His judgement, when for a brief moment He is showing me a little sympathy, between one blow and the next? A moment when life's harsh gaze turns away, when its eyes blink shut and the sentence it has given me seems briefly lighter.

My mother was my killer and I am also that woman's victim. That is how I see it. I did not hurt anyone. All I did was raise my arm, ready to ward off the blows. That is not murder.

But I miss my mother very much. I miss her and I long for her. In the night I talk to her, and I cry. 'Mother, why?!' I ask her in my head. If a mother doesn't love her daughter, then who will she love in this world? Mother, why did you change so much as you got older? Didn't I obey you enough? I obeyed you without question, always. Why did you become so harsh, both with me and with my daughter – the girl you snatched straight out of my womb and took away from me, pressing her to your heart? And why did you detest me after my divorce? Why did you want to forget me and erase me from your life? You knew very well why I fled from that man into your embrace, and why I demanded a divorce. Through it all, did you really have to endure more than I did? Why did you find it so easy to see me living a life of evictions and vagrancy, sucked down into the mire of servility, and all but choking to death in the sludge?

Was I supposed to seek some kind of absolution? What was my sin?

I can't believe that it was all simply about money. And your greed.

What I keep saying to myself, in my head, is that the man who wrote that letter still hopes to meet his mother, and he's trusting in receiving her forgiveness now that he's made a full confession, telling her about his criminal history, all those things he has done with his own two hands. In his letter, he admitted he had no one else, anywhere, and he was standing before her as if he were facing the Creator, submitting willingly to his fate, not shielded by any lies... And so I hope you can hear me from the other world you're in. I hope you will forgive me. I am a mother too, and I know that you love me, that you loved me when I was a child. And then the world treated you harshly. The hardships accumulated, as they did for me, and the bitterness of it all weighed on your heart. This is what life does to us, how it determines things. Life unleashes its storms on us and we are no more than feathers whirling in hurricane winds.

But is it life itself that does this, or is it poverty? Sometimes I have the feeling that God created some people unnecessarily. Beings who live exhausting, useless lives, unneeded by anyone, just like the biting, stinging, harmful vermin the Creator made, who carry diseases and lay their eggs on corpses. The Creator's wisdom, no doubt. Flies, cockroaches, despicable creeping insects, like the man who wrote the letter: harmful and loathsome. Like me too.

Service broke me. I became a servant of everything and for anyone. If the servants of this earth had an anthem, I would have memorized it long ago and I would never stop chanting it. God's other creatures, whom He created us to serve, can bite into the sweet fruits of life with their strong white teeth. We don't envy them. We have no hope of ever being like them, in spite of our mouths watering when the juice runs down their chins. But when life treats us fairly we simply become obedient servants, thanking God that we are fit to serve the others.

I look at my daughter, there in front of me. She is alone in this world, as I am too. I have felt more isolated, more a stranger, since she came to be with me. She watches television but her eyes are vacant and wandering. I don't believe she is truly unable to speak. She just wants to torment me, because she hates me. She despises me for what my mother told her: that I had left her. That it was I who caused this situation, that I had abandoned her and wasn't sending enough money for the two of them, even though – my mother said – I was lounging about in luxury. That I lived a life of sin, working as a whore. That is why my daughter wrapped her head in a hijab as soon as we came here. There's no doubt she blames me for bringing her into this world that she hates so much.

I go into the kitchen. I make tea and stand at the window, looking out at the night. I stare into a night whose air is strange and alien, with no home country where it can land in safety. It's a thick, heavy night out there, with droplets of mist that cling to one's eyelids and hands. This is not my life, and I don't know how I slipped into it. I don't know who pushed me into this night, entangling me in this destiny where I have closed all the doors behind me.

My beloved brother, I'm still hiding those stolen things in a secret place. It's a safe place. When you come out of prison, you must put an end to all those doubts and suspicions you have about me. You must stop forcing your harsh words on me. Because now I've told you the truth. All of it. You have to help me dispose of the goods. I'll give you your share of the house and of everything we manage to sell. I have to take care of my daughter, get her into treatment. We'll conduct ourselves as brothers and sisters do, because I don't have anyone else now. On my own, I can't manage things.

I'm not going to send my letter to you by post. Of course not. I'll find some way to get it to you. Or I'll pass it to you in prison during the visit I'm planning to make, a few days from now, or a few weeks, inshallah. Or maybe I should just erase this idea from my head, because it could expose me to serious danger.

They're calling us back to work.

I'll give it all some more thought.

Kisses.

B eloved Father,

We always found it hard to talk. I kept on believing that the love I felt for you would somehow loosen my tongue, even if I kept it to myself.

I used to dream about sitting close to you, taking your hands in mine and leaning my head against your shoulder, telling you things, and then you would tell me things. But life seems to be treating us unfairly, increasing the distance between us, pulling us further apart than ever. What I dread most is the possibility of regret, sorrow over opportunities lost to silence or frittered away in denial, when we finally realize that it is too late, that it is no longer possible for the two of us to come together. May God give you a long life, Papa.

I know how much you love me. After all, I'm the son you waited so long to have. Writing this letter to you today is my way of declaring, in black and white, that I've hidden nothing – you really do know me very well, whatever you might say. There are no terrible secrets between us, no shocking past that I couldn't bear to tell you about face to face, that I could only bring myself to confess in a letter. Whenever I need to convince myself about this, all I have to do is study those photographs where we are close together, as if I were a little piece of your body. Photos in which you are playing with me, or feeding me, or lifting me high overhead, or bending over my bed. Photos where you are laughing, and looking so proud as you show me off to your mother and father; or where you are carrying my satchel on the way to school. Or where we are eating ice cream and I'm crying because it has melted, and it's running all the way down my arm to my elbow.

Ever since I found out about your illness – God willing you will come out of it safe and sound – I've had this recurring dream. My arms are around you, and either the illness is serious enough to put you in danger, or you are, in fact, dying. In the dream, I am twice my actual size and your body is very small, and naked, and curled up like a foetus or shrunken-looking like a large, featherless bird. And so, when I hold you in these dreams I can enfold you completely, bending over you as if I'm the protective barrier keeping some great peril from descending on you. I keep having this dream even though I know that your illness isn't serious and that you're improving steadily. These nightmares won't leave me alone. If I've kept silent about them, it is only because I haven't wanted to give you any more cause for worry than you already have. And also because I don't want these nightmares of mine to lead to a conversation on a topic we have already been over so often. I mean, of course, my *weak personality*. And because, anyway, the more broken and disjointed our words get, the more we try to obscure or evade the truth, the harder and more complicated it is to hold on.

What gave me some courage to write, finally, was a letter written by a woman who was all on her own, lonely and deserted just like me. It's a letter I stumbled across a long time ago in my little storage locker in the bar I worked in. Yes, back then I worked in a bar here – not a restaurant. Most likely she was one of the girls who worked there as a cleaner, or she was a hostess type sitting with the customers. Maybe she stuffed it into my locker to hide it. Probably she was being followed, for reasons she talks about in her letter. But there's no address, no signature. The letter also says that she hid a document belonging to someone else. Whatever it was she hid could well have given rise to further accusations against her. It is too late for that now. So much the better for her.

The point…the point is, I reread that letter, though it's been more than two years since I found it. I read it again and again, as if I knew that woman personally. Or as if I could actually see her in front of me, asking someone's forgiveness but discovering she could not get it. And not just because her letter would never arrive. It's about the need we all have for someone to listen to us, and then to decide they will pardon us no matter what it is we have done. I was a bit shaken when I reread this letter, and I felt some remorse about having forgotten it, there in my pocket, as if I had carelessly but deliberately neglected something that had been entrusted to me. I felt very badly even though I knew perfectly well that the chances of my ever getting that letter to where it was supposed to go were slim to the point of non-existence. As if this were some kind of betrayal, or abandonment. In short, what I did, without having any great hopes, was to go back to that bar and inquire whether anyone had ever asked to see me. No, they said. And the truth was that no one working there back then still worked there now.

What I do want to tell you right away is that somewhere inside I feel so fiercely proud of you. Of your love for us, and your determination to protect us in times of stress, and how ready you were, always, to make sacrifices for us and for what you believed in, then and still. I try always to imagine myself at your age, to put myself into the times you were living through then. But what paralyses my brain is the question of whether I could ever do what you have done in your life. Anyway, it's an impossible exercise to imagine such things, totally impossible. No one can put himself in another's place. What I mean is, in another person's exact place. And in my case there is a crucial detail, which is that my body – which has made me who I am, in my deepest self – is not your body. My body, which you see as a betrayal. I cannot be a fighter because I am not committed in the way that you are – or I am not a true believer, devoutly pledged to the issues you've spent your life defending. What I'm trying to say is that it isn't because I'm a *girlie boy*, as you call me. There are plenty like me who have fought and killed and been killed, and they're probably more savage than the rest. No, it's because combat and killing aren't my style. And in any case, I couldn't do any of it if I wanted to.

When my masculinity, my sex, slipped from my grasp, when I could see how the beloved body of the child I was began to abandon me, taking on the soft fragility and ambiguity that left it offensive, repugnant and unlovable in your eyes…these were the moments when I most needed (desperately needed) to see that you loved me. Or at least I needed to see that you were ready to give me some help to understand what was happening. You saw it as an illness, expecting me to recover fully, to come out of it free and clear with a little shove from the natural processes of growing up, or simply with a dose of time. An illness, but one without the sort of physical pain, for example, that would lead a dad to take his son to a doctor for treatment or to give him over-the-counter painkillers. My 'illness', you thought, was essentially an inadequacy or a deficiency, even if it was also a sign, in your eyes, that I was a depraved and sinful person. At the end of the day, my 'illness' was a punishment, or a retribution, and you searched high and low for what had caused it. A curse from heaven, a pathology, a punishment God brought down on you – on *you* – by visiting it on me?

Your pain caused me pain, a lot of pain. I wished I could just disappear. I begged God, on my knees, to cure me. If it was God who had erred when he'd made me like this, then who else could I go to in search of deliverance? I started to fear you. I wasn't afraid of the weapons you carried nor the guns your men surrounded

145

you with. What scared me was the sharp click of your key in the door; your nakedness when you came out of the bath; your loud laugh; your crude, hurtful jokes and horseplay; your sick, underhanded mistreatment of my mother; all the ways you dominated us, on the pretext that you were just defending the homeland from danger. Every time you came by the house, the blood pulsed in my heart with terror and joy. Every time you left us to go to war, I breathed an enormous sigh of relief and immediately began to cry because you might die in the very next battle you entered.

But I got older, and I got over being a curse or a sickness. Now, I am who I am. Because there are others who have loved me, people other than you. Once again, I began to feel good-looking, comfortable with myself, someone people liked and desired. I've seen God in His compassion, His tenderness, the largeness of His heart. The boy you shoved out of the house with your own hands, claiming it was the hashish – one single hash cigarette – what about him? You spat in his face and called him terrible things, blaming him for becoming a deviant. How old was I then? *Deviance* was your obsession, the spectre you began to see in everyone you encountered and in everything that went on around you. You, who called yourself 'defender of the weak', the outcast and untouchable, the exploited; you, who had fought against oppression and tyranny, as you always said over and over. How many deviants have you killed? How many betrayers have you murdered before they could betray anyone?

Father, one day I watched a documentary about a people who lived in a remote region of Russia, under the czar, somewhere on the border with Siberia. Their creator, their lord, was the raven-god whom they called Kutkh. What was bizarre about this was that they treated their god like one of them. No particular reverence, no exalted status, no worship to speak of. They blamed their god for certain things and they mocked the world this god had created for its deficiencies. They called him 'stupid', because the universe in which we live could be a more agreeable place, our existence easier, and life less harsh and less mean. But still, they did consider him their lord and their creator, in all likelihood because he was close to them, he resembled them, and they could criticize him knowing he would not come back at them with revenge or count it against them or punish them. When the czar's knights – the Cossacks, mounted on their terrifying stallions – reached those people to bring them into the embrace of the Orthodox Church, they butchered and burned and destroyed, and they used the girls and women as oxen, since there were no such beasts in that region. They enslaved whoever was left and then they erected the Church of God under the exalted mercy and blessed benefaction of the czar.

Father, is it the czar who represents God's will on earth? Or might it be the raven? Do the people ever get to choose?

Father, I did not leave because I was fleeing from you, or from the wars in our homeland. I didn't leave in order to continue my studies or improve my future chances, or anything else like that. I fled from the czars, and I followed the raven. I loved the raven, and the raven was all that was left to me. No, I am not an angel. But nor am I a devil. I might be closer to the second, I suppose, if we were to explain what happened to me as some kind of retribution.

As it happened, not long after I met my beloved and began living with him, the symptoms began showing on him. He was no longer able to work. The owner of the fashion boutique where he had a job threw him out. We moved from our small flat to a single room. Then I moved from working in a sandwich shop where I made almost nothing, to a bar in a Jewish neighbourhood where a lot of gays lived. I didn't feel any hesitancy about beginning to sell some of my evening hours to those who wanted a fly-by-night relationship. We needed the money badly. I didn't feel any shame about working as a prostitute. But the treatment we were paying for didn't yield results. My companion – my love – withered away in my hands, a little closer to death with every day that passed. All the care and attention I'd lavished on him weren't any use at all.

When he refused to be moved to the hospital, I had to wash him, to feed him, to find ways to relieve the pain in the pus-filled sores all over his skin that by then was practically just a membrane over his bones. I was like a devout nun bent prayerfully over his many wounds, every evening and every morning. I held him in my arms as though he were a child, and very carefully and softly I rubbed rosewater into his wasting body. I changed his dressings. Even without any adhesive, the new squares of gauze stuck to his skin. I changed the sheets and washed them. I ground and pulped whatever I could in the blender so that I could feed him before going down to dry the sheets in the communal laundry and then making the rounds to buy the supplies we needed. Until he asked me to stop. 'Leave me alone,' he said. 'I'm asking you not to touch me, from now on.' He began pushing my hands away, and he would no longer eat anything at all.

Before long, when I finished work I avoided going up to our room. I would sit on the park bench in the street long enough to fall asleep. One very early morning, at sunrise, a policeman woke me up. He was very kind. 'What's going on, my son?' *My son*, from a city policeman! I started crying as I got up and walked away.

I left him to die alone. That is a fact no matter how much I try to disguise it by using other words. No matter how often I say that I was only complying with his request, indeed his orders; no matter how forcefully I insist that it was his right to refuse to be seen in that state, repulsive and disgusting; still, I left him to die on his own. What I told myself was: when death comes, he won't need anyone there. He will be so weak that he will simply flicker out like a lightbulb. He will not need me when he is dead. He will not need anyone. He has been dying for a long time. And I must forget him, because otherwise I will die along with him.

I got used to the street. The touch of other bodies was a solace I had been needing and searching for. Bodies alive with health and vigour, skin that did not ooze or know pain, unless it was the pain of pleasure.

My strong attachment to lepers and cripples – by which I mean all those people who suffer the illnesses of unwanted solitude and loneliness – turned into a love, a passion and a way of life that nourished me. There are so many of them out there: people whom life has cast mercilessly out to the margins where no one can see them, into the wastelands of isolation, walled off by virtue of their invisibility. These people see no one and no one sees them. Any attempt to infiltrate the world beyond that wall ends in catastrophic, violent repulsion, like the meeting of two substances whose magnetic charges repel each other. Two worlds, completely cut off from each other, two languages whose codes are mutually undecipherable, unreadable in whichever direction you try to read them.

We criss-crossed the streets of the city, sometimes stealing, more often begging, and though it's easy to forget now, laughing and amusing ourselves too. Late in the evenings, I went with them to wherever it was they drank themselves to sleep: on the street corners, under bridges or in homeless shelters when the cold was at its worst. In one of those centres they examined us, and it turned out that I hadn't been infected. I was very happy about that.

Among the people I got to know was a guy who showed up from time to time to preach to us. But he wasn't dull or irritating as priests usually are. He laughed and joked with us. He didn't hold forth with grandiose words about fires or Hell or things like that. He called himself an *evangelist*, a Bible-person; that is, he wasn't part of a church. He read the scriptures and learned what to do from the life of Jesus of Nazareth. We didn't throw him out, not only because he told such entertaining stories, but also because he had connections to various organizations which meant he could bring us a few of the things we needed. Then one day he took me and a handful of the younger lads outside the city to a very nice-looking centre for immigrants. It was like a small hotel. That was where a doctor told me that one of my eyes was going completely blind and that we must take immediate action to treat the other one so that I wouldn't lose both. He said it wasn't anything I had done. It was bacteria spread by a particular species of mosquito that laid its eggs in human eyes. I was very upset and sad, but what could I do? Sad…and angry. Then I began focusing on my hopes to save my one good eye, and did everything the doctor instructed in his weekly visits.

'Why?' I asked the evangelist in one of our evening gatherings where we listened to him telling the stories of the Messiah. 'Why did people – why did all the people – choose Barabbas when Pontius Pilate asked them whom he should free on Passover, Jesus of Nazareth or that thief, that highwayman?' His response was so amusing that we laughed out loud. 'Because the people are not always right.' He was cheating, I told him, because the question really was: 'Why did the people *vote* against Jesus? Why was it in their interest to do that? What was their motive?' Someone else said, 'Jesus already knew what was happening, and it was his decision to go to the cross himself.' 'But why?' asked someone else. The first guy said, 'That's just the way it was.' The evangelist chimed in: 'To sacrifice himself for us, to die for our sakes.' But we protested. 'Then how come we're still dying horrible, painful deaths, even though none of us has sinned?' We went back to laughing and our usual loud bantering as he thought for a bit. And then he said, 'It's a parable. The Scriptures are all about parables and symbols. Do any of you know why the Messiah walked on water?' 'No,' we said. 'No, we don't know.' 'So that the rest of us would attempt the impossible,' he replied.

This idea of walking on the water appealed to me. I looked at the people around me. They had all been rescued, pulled out of the seawater. They had lost their friends and family members to sinking boats. Maybe they should have tried walking on water. They didn't, though, and this must have been due to a lack of faith or a shortcoming in the way they'd been raised. If we were really believers, we would have walked – without any boats, without the dangers and costs of those boats.

I would have put on a pair of comfortable, roomy shoes and walked on the water all the way to Europe. Maybe even further. Hahaha! Or I would have tried to cross on a skateboard, since that's a bit faster than walking. Maybe I would have stopped to have a pleasant picnic on the water – on the blue surface of the sea – followed by a nap. That would have renewed my strength to go on skating across.

And then there was that little strip of cloth covering the crucified man's lower body – why did it never fall off? I asked him this question just for a bit of a laugh. I knew that, back then, when a person was crucified he was left completely naked, to humiliate him. So I said, 'They always crucified people stark naked, since the point was to shame them by uncovering their private parts. So why cover *him*?' It's all very well for paintings and icons and statues in churches to respect the feelings of worshippers and believers. After all, a believer is modest and bashful by nature, and wants to focus on what he's at church for. But these days, they strip us naked for the most trivial procedures. Yallah, take off your clothes! Yallah, everything – take it off! Underpants, too? Yes! As if a person's penis or belly button will reveal secrets if they search it. Anyway, no one's embarrassed now when everything's on show. They're not embarrassed and neither are we.

The evangelist fell back on his parables and his symbols, caught out by the question and unsure if it was asked in seriousness or jest. It all ended with us throwing him out of our gathering, because he couldn't get into the spirit of our teasing. After that evening, I widened my circle of acquaintances. I began to enjoy hearing languages I didn't know. When one of the other immigrants spoke to me in a foreign language I just nodded and smiled, not understanding a word.

For some reason, many of them spoke to me often and for long periods of time. Probably because they knew I didn't understand their languages. They talked to me without actually looking at me. Anyone who wanted to ensure I was taking in what they said would look straight at me and speak in English. Maybe they took me for a madman, or just slightly batty, because of my one-eyed gaze. Maybe that's why, at night, they would start sobbing in my presence, and why they walked about stark naked in front of me, coming from their bath, without showing any sign of embarrassment.

Then suddenly one morning, when we went out for our required exercise, we found the field around our centre choked with small tents of all colours, like wildflowers that had sprouted overnight amid the grass. Then came the buses packed with people – women and children.

The buses disgorged everyone in an area fenced off with barbed wire. At the perimeter there were waves of police patrolling, addressing people through microphones and from behind plastic shields. They were tossing water bottles at them, and bundles of clothes. At one side of the field, TV vans were lined up. I felt dizzy. 'It's spoiled now,' I told myself, and I left.

I'm writing all of this, Father, to tell you that, like the others, I vote for Barabbas, the conscience of the people. And that now, finally, I acknowledge the czar's power. I am homeless these days, just a vagrant with nowhere to go, who is sick and partly blind. I have no money, I have nowhere to sleep. I'm worn out. I want to come home.

I still have my identity papers. If you agree to it, send me the money for a ticket, or send me a telegram c/o the post office at the airport, where I'll post this letter. That's where I'll be, waiting for your answer.

I hope you will answer quickly. Salaam.

PART TWO

Those Who are Searching

Like a mad fool I rushed off to the airport, hoping to find him there.

That man we'd come upon one day, the one whose horrible moustache we mocked, told me he had just seen him hailing a taxi. And that he'd had a large suitcase with him.

I was immediately suspicious when this man claimed to be a relative, which is how he presented himself to me. He was too polite. He said he felt badly for me, because he had seen me on this street before, gazing long and hard up at that window as I walked by. Whatever – I didn't think this was the moment to get into any of the details. Without delay, I flagged down a taxi. I went straight to the departure gates where flights to his country leave from. I waited for hours, like an idiot.

Because…how could I have possibly found him? How could I have believed that impostor on the street? What did he have to gain by lying to me like that? People here are strange. The men are riddled with complexes. They're sick.

I would walk down his street, passing his home, more than once a week. Sometimes the light was on in his room, and then I would sit in the café opposite, with the prostitutes and the pimps, waiting for him to come down to buy something, or just to go for a walk, and then I would make something up. Well, hello, what a coincidence!

Other times I kept watch, studying the curtains, looking for a woman's shadow, one of his many lovers. My basic and most powerful motive was punishment. Getting my revenge. But I wanted to find the right way to do it. An instrument worthy of my hard anger. I needed to come up with a manner of revenge that would be truly painful for him, carving out a hole in his life that he would never be able to overlook, or fill.

I could not satisfy my thirst. In the last few weeks, his window was always dark. I asked his neighbour, the plump prostitute whom I guessed he frequented, and she said she hadn't seen him for a while.

This man was a truly harmful being. Causing pain was in his nature. He was broke and had nothing to lose. He was arrogant and full of himself; he was backward in his ideas and pretentious in his claims, violent with people but always quick to break into tears. As soon as he reckoned I had fallen for him – fallen in love or at least fallen into his bed – the torment began. What he inflicted on me was planned out and methodical. By torturing me, he was trying, most likely, to make me more attached to him, more dependent. That was his sick logic.

In the end I loathed him, and I found all his complexes and problems repulsive. It seems they were all products of a miserable childhood in an ailing country, things he'd carried with him his whole life. His loneliness, the desolation that was primed to play on my sense of sympathy, became an instrument of relentless torment boring into my head. I never saw him in the company of even one friend, never saw him with a relative, and as far as I could tell, he'd never had a lover who stayed with him for more than a week.

Resentment, hatred and some lingering sympathy – together they drove out the all-consuming passion that destroyed years of my life. A combination of anger and pity filled the space my passion had occupied, and then the pity vanished. Revenge was all I could think about. That is what would bring me back to life. The life he had denied me. It would bring me back to men. To love, to sex. I felt as though he had squeezed out all the juices of my soul, that I could never again feel attractive, never again be someone a man might desire. How could that man want me so madly and then, the very same evening, shed me so completely? I would tell myself that it was because he loved me so intensely that he wanted to put me to the test like this. He wanted to make me his patient Job, to treat me as the Lord treated Job, out of His abiding love. He singled out Job to reward him for the goodness of his heart. God said to Job: You are the one, the only one, to deserve everything that I will do to you. I choose you, in your purity, singling you out from all of humanity, for a special, limitless torment. But you will be free! You are not bound by the wager I have made on your love for Me. I will leave it to you to choose whether or not the bet is lost. However, the story will never be over unless and until I win the bet... Ah, the wisdom of proverbs, legends and fables, the stories we tell.

He chose me, in my purity, for his torture. Other women he had been with he abandoned, allowing them to go away whole, in peace, with a fond farewell, probably expressing some humility and gratitude. Except me... except me. It is almost as though he *had* to keep bringing me back, as if he were sentenced or condemned to retrieve me from wherever I had managed to flee – if I managed it, that is. He would search high and low for me, bringing me back only to fling me further away.

What obsesses me now is my stupidity. Why did I keep going back to him, and how could I have been led on so blindly by his promise to keep me and take care of me, to make amends, compensating me for my strong powers of endurance, my ability to hide the ulcerations in my heart, my failure to make him take responsibility for my affliction, my illness. Because it got to the point where I became as sick as he was, and it was the same kind of sick. It was too much, I couldn't bear it. The route I had to take to get to him was now so terrible, so ugly, that I no longer wanted to arrive. I no longer wanted his passion. I no longer wanted Job's prophesying. All I wanted was to wallow in my own open wounds, and I didn't want to see them close up. Sickened as I was, I could control my passion for him. And as long as I knew him, the passion consumed me; it didn't leave me any room for healing – nothing to give me the strength to reject this sickness.

He disappeared. I had believed that love made all masks fall, that love was the truth, as they taught me through the words of the Messiah. But it seems to me now that one enormous mask covers the body of the world; or that the world is only a massive accumulation of masks over masks, with nothing beneath them in the end. And that I am blind.

I sit down in an out-of-the-way bank of seats to hide the streaks of tears on my face from passers-by. But what I want to do is to scream at them. What is the problem? What's the matter with my crying? Why should there be anything strange about it? Aren't airports places made for saying goodbye? For tears?

I blow my nose and take a deep breath. If my father were alive, I would have gone to him. My father was the only man anywhere to whom I could have asked my questions: where did that man disappear to? How could he leave me without a word? What did he want from me?

What did he want?

Father, help me. Were his loneliness and alienation my doing? What did I not attempt for his sake? Why did my heart attach itself so strongly to him? Alone, and knowing he was far away, sometimes, suddenly, I have felt his head next to mine. In the bus, for instance. Then I'd start shivering and it would always end in a bout of tears. Why? Why have I found myself fixating on some man, any man, who looks just slightly like him from the back, and then following him for hours when I know perfectly well that it isn't him there ahead of me? Did he ever love me, for even a day? A moment? In the café, in the street, in his bed? Is it just that I reminded him of some woman he did love, and he saw her in me? Or was I like his mother, whom I imagine he really did despise, so deeply that he never allowed even one question on anything that was remotely connected to her?

But mightn't his disappearance be against his will? Did he have enemies I didn't know existed? It seems very unlikely that he would have returned to his country without saying a single word about it, not ever, even as a remote possibility. Especially once he was working on getting back his passport. That's what I believe. Because, in the end, we had become friends. Or at least we would have...

Did he get his passport back? I'm not certain. He told me a lot of lies. Yes, he lied to me so often. I moved through his sets of lies as though I were moving through a rainstorm and trying to dodge every raindrop. There were so many lies that I couldn't even remember to ask myself, between one lie and another, whether there was any speck of truth in what he was saying. The next lie would be upon me before I had taken in the last one. It got to the point where I was convincing myself that all the energy he poured into constructing these huge edifices of falsehood, with such careful engineering, was proof of how much he loved me. The love of weak, empty, failed people.

I go back to my ghosts. I think about how he tamed me the way animal trainers at the circus tame bears. And about how I accepted it. I took it all, without even demanding or expecting a single cube of sugar. Then he trained me up with obstacle races. Every time I jumped over a barrier he piled on ten more. And I went along with it. I took it all, even though I had nothing to show for it, not even a tin-plate medal! Maybe in his sick mind he truly believed it gave me pleasure. A kind of delectable masochism. Maybe he was right. Maybe he saw in me something I couldn't see in myself. If it weren't so, then why did I take it?

It was as if I opened my thighs and my heart to the wind, to a ghost, to the shadow of a man. The longer he looked at me, the more transparent I seemed to become, the more absent to his eyes. When he slept with me, it was like he was consuming me, a ripe and tasty piece of fruit, and then he tossed me away like the pit that was left behind, like the fruit's rotting remains, already poisonous. What did I have that he loved, and what did he hate? Was he afraid of me? Did he have secrets, dangerous ones?

Did he go to another woman, one who loved him more than I did? Then why would he hide her when he knew that I would not have put any obstacles in his way? What right would I have had? Because he had long let me know that I had no rights over him, and I accepted that. And I consented to humiliations much more painful than this. I wanted him to feel reassured. For his sake I turned into a different woman. I put up uncomplainingly with things no woman from his country would endure. Maybe I should have done the opposite of that. Or maybe the important thing was that I not resemble them. I don't know. I no longer know anything.

I no longer know anything but this consuming hate. Nothing but the violence of my desire for revenge. To the point of murder. To kill him with my own hands.

I was here. Finally I was in the airport, but only after a long delay. Over there, we'd waited for more than ten hours before taking off, and then six hours in the aeroplane, and then we landed.

I was unbelievably exhausted. The hotel was about a hundred kilometres away. That would mean an hour's taxi ride, assuming we hit no traffic on the way. And it was raining, so we would make slow progress no matter what.

My suitcase still wasn't on the conveyor belt. Probably lost; that wouldn't surprise me. And then it would be days before they came across it; likely they wouldn't locate it before I was back in Canada. The bag's delay added another layer of nuisance when I was already fatigued beyond belief, tipping my exhaustion into anger and bitterness.

Why hadn't I packed a smaller case, one that could go into the overhead locker, as I normally did? Was I perhaps imagining that I would stay a week, or more? It's strange how the logic shuts off in our heads sometimes.

What to do now? I wondered, with this airline employee hovering, asking me to fill out a form in the lost luggage office or else to stay here and wait. To wait until someone finds my bag here inside the sorting and distribution area. He goes on and on, explaining the state of chaos across all airports today due to the storms. Completely dazed, I'm utterly worn out, my mind refusing to work.

I had sat down in the waiting area, having returned my luggage cart. The electric belt on the carousel stopped moving. Then passengers coming from somewhere else began collecting around it.

I remembered that my medications were in the outer pocket of my bag. I had taken out only what I would need to get me through the flight, leaving the rest in that zipper pocket. Why did I do that? The medications didn't weigh much, and I could have put them in my little shoulder bag along with my tickets.

Why…why?

Why am I here? What made me leave my house on a night when there were storms raging everywhere? Was it just to have some fun? A little flirtation, a bit of a joke? To see a woman I knew when she was a teenage girl? Was it some kind of fatal curiosity? Or a test of the old masculine magic? Of the charm I had when I was still young and vigorous and something to look at? Then: Why not? I had said to myself. Why not go and see? I'm not ready to surrender completely to the daily routine of my life. This is the sort of thing we read in novels with feel-good happy endings. This is what seduces us in the films we watch, no matter how scientifically minded we think we are. Film images deposit something in our blood, a poison that settles there, where no medical test can find it.

'Why not?' What a terrible expression. It can lead you to self-destruction precisely because it sounds so playful. Just a game! But when you play a game, you can lose. It isn't appropriate for me to be doing this. It's no longer appropriate. I've been acting as if it's possible to retrieve that illusion of adventure after its time is long gone. When I was young, I circled half the globe. At twenty, I gave up my studies for an entire year and travelled the world. That's how I met this extremely pretty girl. I remember enjoying her, but likely it was just me enjoying myself, being a young man. Probably I did rather fall in love with her, as so often happens at that age. Anyway, life has not been unkind to me. I've had my fair share. I married the woman of my dreams, I came out with an excellent degree and I've had a fine career. So, what is it that I want now, when my joints can't even manage a stroll further than the next bend in the road, as my daughter always says when she wants to get a reaction out of me? Is what I'm feeling simply distress about my advancing age? Can such an unsettled, disturbing feeling as this come over one suddenly, as if from nowhere? Or is it that my enthusiasm has suddenly collapsed, just because my bag is delayed, or maybe even lost?

Or perhaps it's that this idiotic romanticism of mine, which has made me go soft in the head, is no longer up to the fatigue of travelling now that it's no longer fuelled by the old books and films we once obsessed over. It has been decades since I read a romance novel or watched a sentimental film. Where has she returned me to, this woman, this long-ago girl? What trap has she led me into? We are jolted back into our sensible reality when we have to pick ourselves up off the sofa and open the door. The familiar sofa where our worn-out bodies quickly, happily, recognize the barely perceptible depressions they've made there over the years, and the door we close and lock behind us, coming home, as if that locked door will fend off all the horrors of the outside world, its nightmares and its dangers.

It's age. We waited too long, she and I. We were too late.

I am certain now that she has not come. It's out of the question that she would really have travelled all the way here from her home country, once she had given it some thought. And I'm certain she did give it some thought, and then she thought better of it. She wouldn't have let the fantasies tear through her head as they have done through mine.

On the other hand, she did say – that is, she wrote – that if she left her home and travelled to meet me here, in this city, then most likely she would not go back, because she had more travelling to do. Why would she have said that? What travelling did she mean? Or was she trying to tell me that this would just be a passing encounter, that she was not going to attach herself to me or try to hold on to me, that she wasn't looking for anything from me?

But now I'm thinking that these reassuring words could simply be a deception. A trap. After all, what do I know about this woman? For instance, why not consider the possibility that she is on the run after committing some awful crime? Or, what if this brief tryst with her turns out to be like a grain of sand that, regardless of its tiny size, could get inside of me and bring the whole machinery of my life to a halt? In her head, of course, I am still that romantic youth, the adventurous one who travelled without any luggage. She cannot possibly gauge how much I have changed, and how remote I am now from that boy she met.

It's not me, really, who has changed. It's the world and everything about it. That region I criss-crossed far and wide without ever finding anything to fear, where I met people who fed me and gave me shelter, or else slept out in the open, peacefully and without any worries… would I travel to those places now? Certainly not! It would be impossible even to try.

Where was it crouching, all the resentment and hatred? The terrible violence? Back then, I didn't feel the tremors. The peak may have crowned a volcano, but all I saw was a summit covered in snow. Like all the tourists, probably.

Now, whenever I see the apocalyptic images coming from there, on the news or in documentaries, it feels as if I never actually went to those countries. Of course, these images aren't just stories or legends. But to understand what is going on over there, you'd have to devote the kind of effort and time that normal people don't have. Those who do take the time are people driven by feelings of guilt, which are pointless. Nothing ever comes of it, apart from yet another drummed-up cause for romantic young people who don't have a cause. If any of them did decide to get to know that obscure world 'close up', they would return to their family as a few random body parts in a little wooden chest – if they came back at all, that is.

That's what I say to my daughter, who accuses me of the white man's indifference. She says it teasingly but she's half serious. 'But you were there,' she says, over and over again. 'How could you not know anything about those people?'

I didn't know anything before, back then. And I don't know any more now. And here I am in a faraway city with the aim of meeting a woman from that world.

How well can we ever know people who have lived through civil wars? How much can we ever really know about the violence and destruction, the losses, the devastation? The overpowering fear they must feel every day? Can we ever really understand how they are transformed, which things change inside them, and which things harden? In the last quarter of one's life, when death becomes something intensely near and possible, the heart is no longer anything more than a useful pump. Warm blood rushes into our organs only in order to flee once again. There's no other reason, just flight. Coming and going. No feelings, no memories, no... What does she want to escape, that woman I used to know?

The employee is here again, telling me to come and identify my bag. Suddenly I feel more in control of myself. I'll go to the nearest hotel, one of the airport hotels, and tomorrow I'll get on the first flight home.

I am certain I will sleep soundly, and I wish her a good night too, wherever she is.

I hope I can sleep soundly.

I miss the smell of my wife's neck.

They picked me up off the street and dragged me away by force. I carried on kicking and screaming. 'Holy Virgin Mary!' I began calling out. 'Jesus of Nazareth!' I shouted, and shouted that I was an innocent man, swearing by every saint of theirs whose name I could remember. I didn't let up, from the room in the airport police HQ all the way to the door of the aeroplane. I cried and screamed, 'God! What do I have to do with any of this?'

'Where have you hidden your papers?' they were asking me. 'If, that is, you even have residence documents, or papers certifying your refugee status, as you claim?'

I told them, and I swore to it, that I was still waiting for my documents.

'So then, where is the receipt confirming they received your application, the notice you got allowing you free movement?'

I gave them my word that it had been destroyed along with the rest of my belongings when the reception camp burned to the ground. They talked about it in the news. The whole world saw dozens of images of the camp in flames. 'I swear to God, I'm not lying! I was about to submit a request for replacing lost documents. By God, by God, I swear it!'

They laughed at me; they were mocking and sarcastic. They had heard this story many times, they said. Then they announced that my friend had confessed everything after they'd arrested him following that appalling crime. 'He gave us all the details. What he did, and then what you did. It's big, your part in it, very big. The two of you – killing a citizen, a woman who took you in as refugees. You robbed her and cut up her body. There are still some body parts we haven't found. Like the heart. Did you eat that woman's flesh? And you all wonder why people are so afraid of you and why they hate all of you? *C'mon* – everyone back to their own country!'

'God, I had nothing to do with it. I swear to God!'

'We have many witnesses who can identify you. Plenty who saw the two of you together. Lots of them. Stop fooling around! Either you confess or you go back to Albania, where they're even better at getting answers out of people like you than we are.'

I try to lie. I'm lying because I have no choice. Maybe they'll believe some of it, some bit of it. I'm in quicksand and I'm sinking, and soon I will suffocate.

And when I cry out again, sobbing and blubbering that they will kill me there, they ask me, 'Who?' 'Members of a gang I worked for,' I say. 'I was petrified of what they'd do to me if I said anything, but I also kept quiet because I had hopes and plans of my own. So I escaped the gang and then…'

'We're handing you over to the Albanian police. You can tell them all about it when they question you. When they investigate you.'

How could that raging lunatic Arab do this to me? Just because I happened to meet him one rainy day in front of a supermarket, he can now sentence me to death without any chance of appeal? For years I've been on the run, all because I was born in a cursed land, and now here I am going to my execution. There's no point dwelling on how different things would be if I were English, for instance, or Australian or Swedish. Would they *investigate* me this way? Sometimes I think I must be the male hyena cub that the female – the mother – rejected. Life threw me out. And after that, no pack of hyenas would ever accept me. What flock of creatures would ever let me in?

'I'm homeless and I'm a bum,' I told them. 'But I'm not a murderer. I may not have the best principles but if I'd known what that criminal planned to do, I would have informed on him.' I told them I'm royalty when it comes to informants. I turned in my own brother, and I stole my mother's last penny in order to escape that place and come here. 'So why,' I asked, 'do you think I wouldn't inform on that Arab if I'd actually known anything?' I told them that all I was asking for was a few minutes of their time, for them to listen to me. If they could hear about the terrible things I really have done in my life, they would be horrified. They'd believe me. If one of them would just listen to me. 'You're condemning me to death,' I said. 'So allow me one last request before I die.'

This world! People of this world, listen to me! *Yahooooo!*

But from this moment on, no one will speak to me or listen to what I have to say. Now, and here, I've been absorbed into the garbage of this foul world we live in, nature's waste, as if I'm an animal's stinking, rotting corpse. That's why they'll dump me into the aeroplane and tie my legs and arms to the seat.

And I've no hope of being allowed to see anyone after I've been sent back there. There, they will whip-drive me from the aeroplane straight to prison. They won't believe anything I say once I'm inside, either. Not about the Arab and not about the gang. Even if they were to give me the time of day, to listen to what I have to say and then to believe it, who would protect me from getting killed on the outside? Why would the security forces give me protection? What use am I to them? I'm nothing but a little mafioso with a pitiful crime record, who fled from their justice only to find myself running from the justice of the country that's thrown me out. I'm nobody.

It's better for me if they don't believe me. Better if they throw me into a locked cell and keep me there. Of course, the gang is perfectly capable of sending someone to assassinate me inside prison. There are no *extenuating circumstances* as far as they're concerned, not when they believe someone has turned on them.

I know them very well, and I did turn on them. They will be very happy to see me come back.

Why did God put that Arab in my way just when I was on the road to repentance? Is it because God rejects my repentance no matter what? Is it because there is no repentance for someone like me who has committed so many sins? Or is God treating me as He treated the prophets He loved? Putting me to the test? On trial?

But what's the use of putting me on trial when I'm already dead at their hands?

I will chase her to the ends of the earth.

Because of her, I lost years of my life. I was an ass to do what I did for her. I considered myself responsible for her, even though she's three years older than I am. Women are a curse, a punishment to the sons of Adam ever since Creation. Just like all the books say. What the books say about them aren't simply made-up stories or a figment of someone's imagination.

I went to prison to defend her honour – that was more or less what it was about. I wanted to accumulate some money, in any way I could, in order to keep her from the muck of the streets, and from the humiliations of

183

service. Otherwise, what does *family* mean? I'm her brother, and it was up to me to keep her respectable. To defend her honour. Her honour, which turned into a stain, a mark of shame and disgrace.

My father died of exhaustion. From fatigue and keeping his head bowed low. His heart stopped suddenly one night. The whole world turned to me and said, 'Now you're the man of the house.' My mother said, 'Your sister is divorced and she's come back home with her girl. You're her father now. Do something.' I did something. I picked up the suitcase they'd prepared for me, and I took it to the destination they named. It was easy. Until God decreed what would be, and the dogs sniffed out what was in the case.

My sister robbed me. News of it reached me while I was in prison. She forged some papers and sold the house. Who would have believed it? And she stole from the woman she was working for, after killing her. They accused the husband.

Who would have believed any of it? My God, what devil invaded her body? Where did she get these ideas, this talent for bluffing? How did she learn how to build such perfect traps? And she destroyed my mother. I'm ready to say that. My mother, who was an invalid, and *she* killed her. She killed her own mother.

What turned her into this sick, twisted thing?

And then, on top of all that, I learned that she was going around with men in public. People don't say to you openly that your sister is working as a whore. She *was* working as a whore. This woman is not my sister. By God, I swear I don't know her!

There's no doubt that she's fled. She must have left this country for 'an unknown location', as they say. I haven't found a single trace of her. She vanished and no one has any idea where she is. But I will find out everything. Back there, where we're from. I'll find traces of her there. She can't disappear completely like this when she still has a daughter there. Even that criminal murdering whore will return for the sake of her daughter, now that my mother has died. The girl doesn't have a father to go to. Her father remarried, and long ago he stopped wanting the girl.

I will put everything right once I'm there, beginning with getting the house back. After that, I will start searching for her and I'll go on until I find her, and then I'll kill her. I will slit her throat the minute I find her.

Yaah!

She sentenced me to this. She left me no choice. When we were little, she was my gentle, loving, pretty sister. She gave me food, taking it out of her share. She went out to face the older boys in the street whenever she heard the sound of my crying. She took me by the hand and led me to the shop and let me choose whatever I wanted, and she paid for it out of the few coins in her pocket. When the cane swung, she was the one who shielded me from the blows, and she cried when my father punished me. She would take me in her stubby little arms, wash my face and get me to laugh. I would go to curl up by her side, close to her heart, while she told me stories, repeating them as many times as I wanted, letting me play with her braided hair until I dropped off to sleep.

Oh my God… God, tell me where this little girl went? Where did she go, my sister? Where is she? How can I run from this horror into which she has sunk me? And where would I go anyway? Where can I go, now that I've borrowed the money I need for the ticket?

Where?

H ave you received a telegram addressed to me?

No? Thank you.

Has a plane ticket been sent in my name?

No? OK, thank you.

Did a telegram come for me?

Could it have been sent to another post office in the airport?

No? Thank you.

Have you got a plane ticket with my name on it?

Could it have been sent by mistake to another company office somewhere else, other than the airport?

No? Thank you.

PART THREE

Those Who are Left Behind

The dogs in those villages always used to chase me, coming as far as the village graveyards. I was especially careful around some of them, like the wild strays, who were always hungry. I began carrying items in my bicycle basket that I could use to distract them from chasing and biting me, because eventually my legs couldn't take any more bites. I'd got older, and being older, dodging the dogs was not the fun and games it had been when I was very young.

But I still loved my job. I was certain that when I was forced to retire I would become a sad and miserable old man forgotten by all the people I had served. They would no longer remember my rounds, how I always came by at the same time of day; no one would be waiting for me any more. People always used to appear in their doorways, standing on the threshold when they heard the high-pitched screech of my bike, *tireeng-tireeng-tireeng!* Still a good distance away, I could see them raising their hands, signalling to me: 'Any letters today?' The families of young men who had emigrated, newly wed lovers – I mean, the brides left at home when their new husbands travelled to the Gulf – these were always the first to come out of their homes. My delight at handing them letters was as great as theirs at taking them. Recorded cassettes only needed to be slipped into players; but when it came to written letters, I would stay to read them out loud – not always, but when I knew that the letter's recipient couldn't read.

I drank coffee at home with them. They knew I preferred it 'sugar light'. When the envelopes or parcels included a couple of gifts or some sweet treats, there was always a share for me. My postal round ended at the shop, and from start to finish it was always a happy outing. Except when I was bringing news of death. Although even then I was welcomed, for what responsibility does the bearer of news have for its contents?

In our remote district I was treated like a prince. Wherever my bicycle stopped, there was a warm welcome to be had: people invited me in to share their meal, or if not that, they practically forced their home baking on me. The best was fresh loaves of bread still hot from the oven.

I'm not talking about a distant past, not at all! Neither the internet nor anything else could do away with the need for my rounds, not even after internet cafés were springing up everywhere like mushrooms. That was because people couldn't obtain computers easily. They were very expensive and the connection was always dropping out. Plus, it was monitored by the government, who, I should add, were probably responsible themselves for cutting the internet connection. In any case, on a computer no one could afford to write anything that might not please certain people. Or perhaps it was just that they were afraid and so imagined that the government were watching everything. No doubt even the air that bore the currents of electricity was being monitored. But a letter or a cassette – those were almost never targets of surveillance, since the authorities had begun to assume that only backward people used such methods to communicate any more. People whose minds would never turn to terrorism anyway.

And then suddenly I was just a post office bureaucrat, no rounds, no distributing anything. It was because of the wars, these conflicts and battles that dropped on us from the skies, or, more accurately, that rose from Hell; no one understands how any of it happened, or why. Daesh. 'Daesh!' they call out, and people start fleeing and dying in the road, or hiding themselves in enclosures meant for animals. Even the animals scatter into the deserts looking for food, or they're eaten by people who find them already dead. I fled too, several times, but I came back to pick up my salary – that's when salaries were still reaching the office, if not always quite on schedule.

At that time, that's all I was doing. Fleeing and coming back. Getting out, going from one place to the next and back again. The indignity of it all. Coming back here, listening to music whenever I could find batteries for the cassette player. The door to the office had been ripped off its hinges and there was no longer even a single employee left. Had I a wife or children I wouldn't have been able to go away and come back like this. I mean, imagine it, leaving them in camps or on the side of the road, and then never finding them again, anywhere, no matter where I looked in God's wide world. Sometimes, turning it over in my mind, I think I won't live to see the end of Daesh. Or whatever – Daesh or something else. The wrath of the Lord will not be pacified before I die. My life is over now.

I often think about all the lost letters that haven't reached the people they were meant for, letters that are piling up in corners here and there, while the senders have no idea what has happened to them. Like the piles of dead leaves spilling over the kerbs at the corners of deserted streets. Maybe they've started burning them now. People must have begun to realize there is no hope that letters they've written will reach their destinations. Maybe they are no longer even writing any letters. When scores of addresses have vanished in neighbourhoods that are destroyed now, and our empty villages are turning into desert, who do you write to? What address do you use? When the fighting finally comes to an end, they'll have to search very hard to find the street names, or maybe they'll give the streets new names, as victors always do after seizing control of a place.

I've given serious thought to emigrating to where my brother is. That is, if he himself hasn't left the address I have for him. But first I need a postman – hahaha! – to bring me my official papers. They might or might not still be in the house, I don't know. At the moment, I'm living in the post office. I come and go from here. I can't go anywhere near the neighbourhood where my house is. Most likely it has been burned to the ground anyway. But how long will I be able to stay here? These wars jump from place to place, and it's impossible to tell which direction they're going and where they'll be next. The fighter who is a defeated man today will likely return fiercer and more destructive than anyone else tomorrow. He could come back and attack you just when you assume he is fleeing after his latest defeat. All the news I hear on the radio seems to be old news, and so it isn't helpful at all. In fact, my ears tell me how wrong it is, since I pick up the roar of explosions and the drone of aircraft overhead just as the radio announcer is telling me that the war has moved elsewhere.

That's why I only listen to songs now. My attention is mainly taken up with making my meals, which gets harder by the day. The boredom is really getting to me too, now that I've finished reading and sorting all the letters I found abandoned here. I've made a sort of register listing all of them, and I've put the letters themselves together in files that are clearly labelled according to address and date. Someone might come back; the post office employees might return and want to get those letters to the people they're addressed to. Every letter is stapled to its envelope, and the file indicates its level of importance, and whether it is urgent. I even decided to add notes, where an address might be too vague or unclear for anyone who hasn't already worked the postal routes around here.

Now I'm finishing my own letter – it's for whoever might show up here. I'll put it in plain sight, next to the register of letters I've made. Because I might die before anyone reaches this post office.

Who knows?

Author's Acknowledgements

Special thanks go to the Institute for Advanced Studies at the Central European University in Budapest, and to its director, Professor Nadia al-Baghdadi.

Translator's Acknowledgements

Marilyn Booth wishes to thank Helen Szirtes for her sensitive and thoughtful copy-editing.

Oneworld, Many Voices

Bringing you exceptional writing
from around the world

The Unit by Ninni Holmqvist (Swedish)
Translated by Marlaine Delargy

Twice Born by Margaret Mazzantini (Italian)
Translated by Ann Gagliardi

Things We Left Unsaid by Zoya Pirzad (Persian)
Translated by Franklin Lewis

The Space Between Us by Zoya Pirzad (Persian)
Translated by Amy Motlagh

The Hen Who Dreamed She Could Fly by Sun-mi Hwang
(Korean) Translated by Chi-Young Kim

A Perfect Crime by A Yi (Chinese)
Translated by Anna Holmwood

The Meursault Investigation by Kamel Daoud (French)
Translated by John Cullen

Laurus by Eugene Vodolazkin (Russian)
Translated by Lisa C. Hayden

Masha Regina by Vadim Levental (Russian)
Translated by Lisa C. Hayden

French Concession by Xiao Bai (Chinese)
Translated by Chenxin Jian

The Sky Over Lima by Juan Gómez Bárcena (Spanish)
Translated by Andrea Rosenberg

Umami by Laia Jufresa (Spanish)
Translated by Sophie Hughes

The Hermit by Thomas Rydahl (Danish)
Translated by K. E. Semmel

The Peculiar Life of a Lonely Postman by Denis Thériault
(French) Translated by Liedewy Hawke

Three Envelopes by Nir Hezroni (Hebrew)
Translated by Steven Cohen

Fever Dream by Samanta Schweblin (Spanish)
Translated by Megan McDowell

The Invisible Life of Euridice Gusmao by Martha Batalha
(Brazilian Portuguese) Translated by Eric M. B. Becker

The Temptation to Be Happy by Lorenzo Marone
(Italian) Translated by Shaun Whiteside

Sweet Bean Paste by Durian Sukegawa (Japanese)
Translated by Alison Watte

They Know Not What They Do by Jussi Valtonen (Finnish)
Translated by Kristian London

The Tiger and the Acrobat by Susanna Tamaro (Italian)
Translated by *Nicoleugenia Prezzavento* and Vicki Satlow

The Woman at 1,000 Degrees by Hallgrímur Helgason
(Icelandic) Translated by Brian FitzGibbon

Frankenstein in Baghdad by Ahmed Saadawi (Arabic)
Translated by Jonathan Wright

Back Up by Paul Colize (French)
Translated by Louise Rogers Lalaurie

Damnation by Peter Beck (German)
Translated by Jamie Bulloch

Oneiron by Laura Lindstedt (Finnish)
Translated by Owen Witesman

The Baghdad Clock by Shahad Al Rawi (Arabic)
Translated by Luke Leafgren

The Aviator by Eugene Vodolazkin (Russian)
Translated by Lisa C. Hayden

Lala by Jacek Dehnel (Polish)
Translated by Antonia Lloyd-Jones

Bogotá 39: New Voices from Latin America
(Spanish and Portuguese) Short story anthology

Solovyov and Larionov by Eugene Vodolazkin (Russian)
Translated by Lisa C. Hayden

In/Half by Jasmin B. Frelih (Slovenian)
Translated by Jason Blake

What Hell Is Not by Alessandro D'Avenia (Italian)
Translated by Jeremy Parzen

Zuleikha by Guzel Yakhina (Russian)
Translated by Lisa C. Hayden

Mouthful of Birds by Samanta Schweblin (Spanish)
Translated by Megan McDowell

City of Jasmine by Olga Grjasnowa (German)
Translated by Katy Derbyshire

Things that Fall from the Sky by Selja Ahava (Finnish)
Translated by Emily Jeremiah and Fleur Jeremiah

Mrs Mohr Goes Missing by Maryla Szymiczkowa (Polish)
Translated by Antonia Lloyd-Jones

In the Shadow of Wolves by Alvydas Šlepikas (Lithuanian)
Translated by Romas Kïnka

Humiliation by Paulina Flores (Spanish)
Translated by Megan McDowell

Three Apples Fell from the Sky by Narine Abgaryan (Russian)
Translated by Lisa C. Hayden

Little Eyes by Samanta Schweblin (Spanish)
Translated by Megan McDowell

Hoda Barakat is the author of six novels and two plays. Her work has been translated into several languages and received numerous prestigious prize nominations. Her fifth novel, *The Kingdom of This Earth*, (2012) was longlisted for the International Prize for Arabic Fiction in 2013, which *Voices of the Lost won* in 2019. In 2015, she was shortlisted for the Man Booker International Prize (at the time awarded in recognition of an author's body of work). Born in Lebanon, she currently lives in France.

Marilyn Booth is Khalid bin Abdullah Al Saud Professor of the Study of the Contemporary Arab World, University of Oxford. Her literary translations include *Celestial Bodies* by Jokha Alharthi, winner of the 2019 Man Booker International Prize.